The Other Devil's Name

The Other Devil's Name

E. X. Ferrars

FELONY & MAYHEM PRESS • NEW YORK

All the characters and events portrayed in this work are fictitious.

THE OTHER DEVIL'S NAME

A Felony & Mayhem mystery

PRINTING HISTORY
First UK edition (Collins): 1986
First US edition (Doubleday): 1986

Felony & Mayhem edition: 2021

ISBN: 978-1-63194-254-9

Manufactured in the United States of America

Library of Congress Cataloging-in-Publication Data

Names: Ferrars, E. X., author.
Title: The other devil's name / E.X. Ferrars.
Description: New York : Felony & Mayhem Press, 2021. | Series: A Felony &
    Mayhem mystery | Summary: "When a friend consults Professor Basnett about a
    blackmail plot, further investigation reveals a surprising cluster of disappearances
    in a small Berkshire village"-- Provided by publisher.
Identifiers: LCCN 2021007325 | ISBN 9781631942549 (trade paperback) | ISBN
    9781631942556 (ebook)
Subjects: LCSH: Basnett, Andrew (Fictitious character)--Fiction. | Retired teachers-
    -England--Fiction. | Botanists--England--Fiction. | GSAFD: Mystery fiction.
Classification: LCC PR6003.R458 O84 2021 | DDC 823/.912--dc23
LC record available at https://lccn.loc.gov/2021007325

The icon above says you're holding a book in the Felony &
Mayhem "British" category. These books are set in or around
the UK, and feature the highly literate, often witty prose that
fans of British mystery demand. If you enjoy this book, you
may well like other "British" titles from Felony & Mayhem
Press.

———◆◆◆———

For information about British titles or to learn more about Felony
& Mayhem Press, please visit us online at:

www.FelonyAndMayhem.com

Other "British" titles from

FELONY&MAYHEM

MICHAEL DAVID ANTHONY
The Becket Factor
Midnight Come
Dark Provenance

ROBERT BARNARD
Corpse in a Gilded Cage
Death and the Chaste Apprentice
The Skeleton in the Grass
Out of the Blackout

SIMON BRETT
Blotto, Twinks and the
 Ex-King's Daughter
Blotto, Twinks and the
 Dead Dowager Duchess
Blotto, Twinks and the
 Rodents of the Riviera
Blotto, Twinks and the
 Bootlegger's Moll

CAROLINE GRAHAM
The Killings at Badger's Drift
Death of a Hollow Man
Death in Disguise
Written in Blood
Murder at Madingley Grange

ELIZABETH IRONSIDE
The Accomplice
The Art of Deception
Death in the Garden
A Very Private Enterprise

MAGGIE JOEL
The Second-Last Woman in
 England
The Past and Other Lies

SHEILA RADLEY
Death in the Morning
The Chief Inspector's Daughter
A Talent for Destruction
Fate Worse than Death

LESLIE THOMAS
Dangerous Davies:
 The Last Detective

L.C. TYLER
The Herring Seller's Apprentice
Ten Little Herrings
The Herring in the Library
Herring on the Nile
Crooked Herring

The Other Devil's Name

Chapter One

It was nine o'clock on a Wednesday morning in May, and Andrew Basnett, who had been out late the evening before and had overslept, was in his kitchen, dressed in pyjamas, his dressing gown and a pair of socks, and was making coffee for his breakfast when the doorbell rang.

Assuming that it was the postman, trying to deliver a package that would not go through the letter box, Andrew went to the door and opened it.

It was not the postman. It was Andrew's old friend and colleague Professor Constance Camm, F.R.S., whom it was very surprising to find at his door at that hour of the morning.

Now that she was retired, she lived with her sister in the village of Lindleham in Berkshire, and on the occasions when she wanted to meet Andrew, usually made careful arrangements by telephone several days beforehand. She would then probably invite him to lunch with her at her club, or after some persuasion might allow him to take her out to lunch at one of his favourite Soho restaurants. She had only rarely visited the flat in St. John's Wood, where he lived, and then never at such an early hour.

He felt embarrassed on seeing her, not only because she had caught him in pyjamas and dressing gown and still unshaven, but mostly because he was without slippers. When he was alone in his flat he usually padded about it in his socks, leaving his slippers wherever it had occurred to him to kick them off. Today they were on the rug in the middle of his sitting room, and the first thing that he did on bringing her into the flat was to dart to where he had left them and put them on.

After that he felt better.

"I'm sorry to turn up so early, Andrew," she said. "I tried to get in touch with you yesterday evening, but I think you were out, and I've got to get home today as early as possible because I've left Mollie in rather a state." Mollie was the sister with whom she was living in Lindleham. "We've both been feeling very upset and I thought that what we needed was some sound advice and that you were the best person to turn to. If you don't feel you can face that, however, I'll go away. Only I do think it's rather urgent and that you might perhaps be of great help to us."

It astonished Andrew to be asked for advice by Constance Camm. She was as independent a person as he had ever known. She had given him advice at many times in his life, particularly when he had first been appointed to the chair of botany in the London college where he had spent the last twenty years of his working life and in which she had held a research professorship since a few years before his arrival. They were about the same age, which was seventy-one, and had retired at the same time, Constance leaving London after a while to join her sister and apparently giving up all interest in science, while Andrew had remained in his St. John's Wood flat and had devoted himself, in a slightly haphazard way, to writing the life of Robert Hooke, the noted seventeenth-century natural philosopher and architect.

Pursuing this work meant making frequent visits to the library of the Royal Society in Carlton House Terrace, which at least had the virtue of taking him out of his flat. Yet hard as it seemed to him that he worked at the book, it had a mysterious way of appearing never to grow any longer. Perhaps this was because as he went along he kept tearing up most of what he had written a week or so before. If anyone asked him how the book was going he always replied that it was going splendidly, but at the back of his mind there lurked a suspicion that it might never be finished.

This did not disturb him very much. In an occasional mood of depression he might deplore the futility of what he was doing, but luckily such moods were infrequent with him.

"I was just going to make some coffee when you rang," he said. "I expect you'd like some too. So if you don't mind waiting while I get some clothes on, I'll make it and then you can ask me for that advice, which I don't suppose for a moment I'll be able to give you. Here's a copy of *The Times* you can look at while I'm doing it."

"Don't bother to get dressed on my account," Constance said. "You're perfectly decent as you are. But coffee would be nice."

She accepted the copy of *The Times* as she sat down in a chair near the electric fire, which had not been switched on because the May morning was sunny and warm, but she showed no sign of wanting to open the newspaper. It occurred to Andrew as he saw her lean back in the chair and give a quiet sigh that she was looking very tired, as if she had not slept much. She was a small woman, slender and neatly made, with straight grey hair cropped close to her small, well-shaped head, somewhat sharp-featured and eyes of an uncommonly brilliant blue.

They were also uncommonly intelligent eyes, and if her features were sharp they were also mobile and expressive. She was wearing a grey tweed suit, plain, not very expensive, but well-fitting. She had been a close friend of Nell, his wife, who had died of cancer ten years ago, and in her restrained, unde-monstrative way was perhaps closer to Andrew than most of his other friends.

However, he felt that he would be more at ease with her if he got into some clothes, so he retired to his bedroom and presently emerged in trousers, a shirt and a pullover and, going to the kitchen, resumed the making of coffee. He was a tall, spare man who did not look as tall as he really was because he had allowed himself in recent times to get into the habit of stooping. He had rough grey hair and grey eyes under eyebrows that were still almost black. Making some toast, he put it with the coffee, cups, butter and marmalade on a tray and carried it into the sitting room.

But just before he did this he paused for a moment. Opening the refrigerator, he took out a slab of cheese, pared off a slice and ate it hastily. There was something faintly furtive about the way that he did this. He hated the idea that he might be thought a diet crank. He always asserted that he could eat anything that was put in front of him. But he did like to start the day with a small piece of cheese. At some time he had been convinced by something that he had been told, or perhaps had read, that it was important on getting up to eat some protein, and it was much less trouble to eat a little cheese than to boil an egg. Yet somehow he would not have liked to be caught doing this by someone as full of ruthless common sense as Constance Camm.

He found her still in the chair where he had left her, looking as if she had not moved.

She smiled as he handed her a cup of coffee and said, "Really I'm sorry to have come calling so early, but I tried telephoning you from my club two or three times yesterday evening; then when I couldn't get an answer I got the idea into my head that your phone might be out of order, so I came out here on the chance of finding you at home after all, and as that was no use, I thought I'd try just once more this morning. Please forgive me." She sipped some coffee. "This is just what I needed."

"I'm always delighted to see you at any time," Andrew said as he sat down with his own cup of coffee. "You know that. Only I can't imagine what I can do for you that can be worth your taking so much trouble."

"It's this." She opened her handbag and took out a letter. "I'd like to know what you make of it."

"You want me to read it?"

"Please."

He took it from her, glancing at the address on the envelope. It was typewritten.

Mrs. Mollie Baird
Cherry Tree Cottage
Bell Lane
Lindleham
Maddingleigh
Berks.

It was a plain white envelope with a Maddingleigh postmark and had been neatly slit along the top. Andrew took out the sheet of paper inside. It was quarto-size flimsy typing paper and had a few lines of typing about halfway down it.

"Don't forget I saw you bury him. I know where the body is. And it can stay there as long as you remember what I said about payments. Don't forget."

Andrew read it through two or three times, drank some coffee, then read the message yet again.

"This came in the post?" he said.

"Yes."

"When?"

"Yesterday morning."

"Mrs. Baird is, of course, your sister."

"Yes."

"Do you know what it means?"

"No. It seems to me a piece of sheer lunacy. But then again, perhaps it isn't. And that's why I brought it to you. I wanted to talk it over with someone—someone I trust."

He caught an odd note in her voice, and looking at her, he saw that she was watching him with unusual anxiety.

"I suppose neither of you has been burying any bodies recently," he said.

"No, Andrew, we haven't."

"Or anything else?"

"What do you mean?" She had an attractive voice, soft but incisive.

"I just wondered if it could be somehow metaphorical," he said. "Both the body and the burying might stand, so to speak, for something else. Otherwise..."

"Yes?" she said as he paused.

"Well, otherwise I don't understand why you aren't satisfied with your own explanation that it's lunacy. It sounds to me as if it's been done by someone who's trying to frighten you, and it sounds to me, too, more probable that it's been done by someone who's slightly mad than by anyone who's got a real hope of blackmailing your sister. Have you any recognizable lunatics in your neighbourhood?"

She must have thought that there was some flippancy in his tone, for she said, "Andrew, I wish you'd take this seriously."

"But I'm taking it very seriously," he said. "Because you must be frightened or you wouldn't have troubled to bring the thing to me. And you haven't answered my question. Have you any neighbour who seems to you even mildly unbalanced? Lunatics can be astonishingly clever at hiding their madness, you know, as clever as criminals may be about hiding their crimes. And the medical profession cooperates with them nowadays. They want them kept in a so-called normal environment, rather than shut away out of sight. But I once knew a psychiatrist whom I really respected, a very gifted chap, who said that the well should be protected from the sick. I know that's not a fashionable attitude nowadays, but I think there's something in it. What I wanted to ask you, however, was whether or not you've been coming into contact recently with anyone who seems to you even a bit odd."

She finished her coffee, gave another sigh, leant back in her chair and answered, "Most people seem to me very odd."

"That's only natural," he said. "It's difficult for you to understand why people should be less talented than you are yourself. But even you must admit there are different standards of oddity. So tell me if there's anyone you suspect of having written this strange missive."

Her eyes, of the unusually brilliant blue that age had not affected, though the face out of which they shone had many wrinkles, dwelt on his face for a moment, but with a look of gazing beyond it, as if she were contemplating something much farther away. Then she shook her head.

"No."

"So what is it you're afraid of?"

"I'm not exactly afraid. But I'm puzzled. And I'm wondering if there's anything Mollie and I ought to do about it. That's why I came to you. I wanted to talk it over, as I said, with someone I trust. Someone who won't try to push us into doing something that may be harmful to someone else. You seemed to me the obvious person."

"Thank you," he said. "But go on."

"Well, does anything strike you about the way that letter's addressed?"

"Only that it's neatly typed and seems to be correct."

"Yet the letter inside doesn't seem to have been meant for Mollie at all."

Enlightenment dawned on him. "Oh, I see. I think I see. You think someone got confused, wrote a letter to someone else and put it in an envelope addressed to your sister, and no doubt wrote her a letter and put it in an envelope addressed to that other person."

"Yes, and you see what that could mean, don't you?"

He considered it for a moment. "I see one thing it could mean, but it seems rather fantastic."

"I believe we may be dealing with a very fantastic situation," she said.

"It could mean that the writer of this letter did see someone burying a body and has been blackmailing that person ever since."

As he said it he hoped that she would reject this suggestion as being indeed too fantastic, for it might mean, he was afraid, that he would shortly find himself becoming involved in a kind of drama which did not appeal to him at all. It had happened to him before, and in his view it was not really the kind of thing that he was meant for. But he was not surprised when he saw her nod.

"Don't you think that's what must have happened?" she said.

He replied reluctantly, "I suppose it isn't impossible."

"But if that's right," she went on, "the question is, what ought we to do about it?"

"Give the letter to the police," he answered immediately.

"No."

"But of course that's what you must do," he said. "If there's the slightest possibility that you're right, you shouldn't lose any time in giving it to them."

"That's just what I don't want to do, Andrew." Her gaze was sharply focussed on his face. "That's why I came to you. I felt I wanted to talk the matter over with someone who wouldn't try to make me do just that and whom I could trust not to go to them on his own with a story about this slightly strange occurrence. And of course you can see why, can't you?"

He leant forward to refill their cups with coffee.

"I'm afraid you think I'm much wiser than I am," he said. "The only reason I can think of is that the letter you think your blackmailer wrote to your sister but posted to the wrong person is something she or you couldn't face letting the police find out about. But that's nonsense."

"Why is it nonsense?" she asked in her soft, precise voice.

He gulped some coffee which was almost too hot to swallow and made him choke for a moment.

"Of course that's what it is," he said when he could speak. "I'm certain neither of you has ever done anything in your lives for which anyone could blackmail you."

"How do you know?"

"Well, you and I have known each other for a good many years, haven't we?"

That was true, but as he said it he recognized inwardly that there were whole areas of Constance's life of which he knew next to nothing. For instance, though he thought it probable that she had had lovers, she had never spoken about them. But even supposing that she had had any number of them, that was not a thing about which she could be blackmailed nowadays. And he could not imagine that she had ever been engaged in any criminal activities. He was sure that she had never forged a cheque, stolen jewellery or valuables from anyone, or, say, run over someone with her car and failed to report it. She was a gifted, loyal, kindly woman of high integrity and any black-mailer who thought that he could extort money from her must be really in a very bad way. And he had no reason to think that her sister was very different from her.

She smiled slightly when he spoke and nodded and said, "Yes, you and I have been lucky in our way, haven't we? Suppose we'd hated one another, what hell we could have made for one another over the years. The academic world isn't famous for loving-kindness. But I don't want to take that letter to the police. I've got my reasons."

"What do you want, then?"

"Rather a lot. You've only to say no, you know, if you don't want to do what I'm going to ask you. I do realize it's a lot, and you may not have time for it, or may simply intensely dislike the idea of having anything to do with it. I was going to ask you if you would come to stay for a little while with Mollie and me in Lindleham and meet some of our neighbours and tell me... Well, you needn't tell me anything if you don't want to. That would be for you to judge. But I believe you've been involved in murder before, haven't you?"

"To my sorrow, yes."

"You see, Mollie and I have rather lost our heads about all this, and we do want help."

He could think of no one who looked less as if she had lost her head than Constance Camm did just then, but he knew her well enough to be aware that whatever turmoil was raging inside her, it would not show.

"So you really believe there's been a murder," he said, "and it was done by someone you know. And someone else you know saw the body being buried and has turned blackmailer. And you're really scared of what may happen next."

"I won't go so far as to say I actually believe there's really been a murder," she answered, "but it's true I'm scared and I can't stop thinking about it. And Mollie's even worse about it than I am."

"And you think if I meet your neighbours I'll be capable of picking out the culprits. I'm very flattered, but, my dear, if you were to put their names in a hat and let me pick one out, I'd be just about as successful. But I'll come to Lindleham if you really want me to."

Her face brightened. "Today?"

"I suppose today is as good a day as any."

It did not take Andrew long to pack a suitcase and to write a note for the woman who came in to clean his flat twice a week to explain his sudden absence. He left it on the kitchen table, made his bed, washed up the breakfast things, left a note with an empty milk bottle at his door, cancelling deliveries till further notice, checked that he had enough money to last him for a few days and rejoined Constance in the sitting room, ready to leave.

While he had been doing these things he had been muttering, half aloud:

> *Lars Porsena of Clusium*
> *By the Nine Gods he swore*
> *That the great house of Tarquin*
> *Should suffer wrong no more…*

It annoyed him intensely that he could not stop himself doing this. It was one of the misfortunes of his life that in his childhood he had had an ability to memorize verse after only one or two readings, and that all of this, especially if it had a strong, jingly rhythm and was about blood, slaughter and all kinds of violence, had remained in his memory ever since. And it had a way of taking possession of his mind whenever there was a threat that it might be filled with something else that he did not want to think about.

At the moment he did not want to think about murder and Macaulay's deplorable ballad helped somewhat in keeping thoughts of it at bay, as well as stopping him trying to decide if Constance Camm, whom he had always regarded as the most well-balanced of women, was beginning to show the first signs of mental deterioration in her old age or had sound reasons for her fears and suspicions.

Her car, a red Volkswagen, was in the street, and it took them about an hour and a half to reach Lindleham. It was only a hamlet, half a mile or so from the village of Clareham, which was about five miles from the old market town of Maddingleigh. The hamlet was built at a crossroads. A small but fine Georgian house was at the corner where the two roads met, and Bell Lane, in which there were several houses, some of them old thatched cottages, expensively modernized, and some of them recently built, branched off on the right.

Farther along the lane, a Victorian mansion, to the original owners of which all the land as far as the main road had once belonged, stood in a fair-sized but neglected garden. The lane wandered on past it through a chequerboard of open meadows and fields yellow with rape, where once there would have been tall hedgerows and the now vanished elms, small woods with a misty covering of bluebells under beech trees and meadowsweet along the ditches.

Visits to the country always aroused a sad nostalgia in Andrew. He had grown up in a village at the foot of the South Downs, but the countryside of his childhood was gone for ever. He attempted not to yield to regrets too easily, for change had to come and might in the end be for the best. If the conservationists had got to work only a few centuries earlier than they had, he and Constance might have met wolves and wild boars on their journey down from London. In fact, apart from the traffic, all that they had met as they passed one of the cottages in Bell Lane was a brown dog that stood at the gate and barked at them ferociously.

Constance and Mollie lived in a small, modern house facing this cottage. There was a flowering cherry by the gate, which had given the little house its name. As Constance turned the Volkswagen in at the gate Mollie came out to greet them. She was a slightly younger, larger and in some way curiously blurred version of her sister. There was a considerable resemblance between them, yet everything that was neat, taut and sharply defined in Constance was rounded, sagging and vague in Mollie. She had a cloud of thin, curly grey hair which on even the stillest day managed to look windblown. Her eyes were blue, like her sister's, friendly and gentle but without any brilliance. Her clothes hung on her loosely, the hem of her skirt uneven, her shoes flat-heeled and heavy and her stockings wrinkled at the ankles.

She had been married briefly when she was young to a man called Martin Baird, who had been killed in the war, and after his death she had been a secretary, then the assistant manageress of a guesthouse, then had helped in a craft shop in Maddingleigh, and eventually had settled down to being the companion of the old woman who had lived in Lindleham House, the Victorian mansion farther along Bell Lane.

Mollie had stayed with her for about fifteen years and at last, about a year before, had been rewarded for her patience and good nature by a considerable legacy. She had then bought the house into which she now welcomed Andrew, having chosen it because after living there for so long she had wanted to remain in Lindleham, and Constance, who had lived in London until then, had joined her there. It had never seemed to Andrew that the two sisters had anything in common, yet he knew that they had a great deal of affection for one another.

They took him into the living room, a long, bright room with a window at each end, plenty of comfortable chairs covered

in flowered chintz, a few pieces of not very interesting repro-
duction furniture, a remarkable number of staring, blank-faced
Staffordshire dogs, the collecting of which was a hobby of
Mollie's, and on the walls some delicate old flower prints, which
were Constance's contribution to the room. There were several
vases of flowers in it, filled with boughs of flowering cherry,
tulips and wallflowers.

"You'll have a drink, won't you, while I get us some lunch?"
Mollie said. "Then I'll make your bed. I didn't get a room ready
for you till I was sure you'd come. Connie said you would, but I
wasn't certain. I was afraid you'd simply feel we were imposing
on you. Connie said you weren't like that, but I rather thought
myself it was what we were doing. It's so good of you to come
and advise us. I suppose it's stupid of us not to be able to make
up our own minds about what we ought to do. Of course,
Connie's shown you the letter." She had a hasty, slightly inco-
herent way of talking.

Andrew said that he had seen the letter.

"And you don't think we're just being hysterical, worrying
about it?"

During the drive down from London, Andrew had begun
to think that possibly that was just what they were, but she was
suddenly looking extremely anxious, and in any case, now that
he was here, he could hardly say that he was inclined to think
that she and Constance might be making a fuss about nothing.

"It can't do any harm to look into the matter," he said.

"Yes, yes, that's how I feel," Mollie said. "Now what will
you have to drink?"

He chose sherry, and she poured it out for him, and a glass
for Constance, then one for herself, which she carried out to the
kitchen, her heavy shoes thumping on the polished floor as she
went.

Constance was looking at him with a faint, sardonic smile.

"Of course, you've begun to think it's all nonsense, haven't
you?" she said. "A practical joke or something. I noticed it about
Pangbourne. You began to be very tactful with me. You'd begun

to wonder if I'm getting senile. Senile dementia. It's hit better people than me, and younger ones too."

"Perhaps I'm the one who's suffering from it," he said. "It's true I'm finding it difficult to take the matter seriously."

"Well, as you said, it can't do any harm to look into it. We'll talk it over properly after lunch. And if you think it's all too boring, I'll drive you home again. Meanwhile, like Mollie, I think it's very good of you to have come and I hope you'll stay at least until tomorrow."

He assured her that that would be a pleasure, and they had more sherry and a little later were called into the dining room by Mollie to eat cold chicken, salad and cheese, and if it had not been for an almost glazed look of worry that from time to time appeared in her mild blue eyes, it would have been easy to forget that it was a strange and surely nonsensical letter about the burying of a body that had brought him there.

But as soon as the meal was over and coffee, made by Constance, had been brought into the living room, the two sisters fell silent, looking at him in an expectant way that made him feel more than a little foolish. It did not altogether surprise him that Mollie, simple soul that she was, should assume that he would be able to help them with their problem, but that Constance should be hoping that he could do so puzzled and disturbed him.

"Now let me get things clear," he said as he accepted his coffee cup. "That letter came yesterday, it was posted in Maddingleigh, and for some reason you believe it was intended for someone you know. And that's the first thing that puzzles me. Suppose you're right that it was put into a wrong envelope and that the letter that was meant for you has gone to someone else, why shouldn't that person live, say, in London, or even abroad? What is there about it that makes you think it was sent to someone in this neighbourhood?"

"We don't, exactly," Constance answered. "That's to say, if it wasn't, then we don't much care where it went. If it went to someone who's never heard of us and can't identify us, then it really doesn't matter and we can forget the whole thing. But there's the address on the envelope, you see. Bell Lane, Lindleham. It seems to us that it would have been easier for this person, whoever he is, to muddle up the two letters if the addresses were fairly alike."

"I see," Andrew said. "I realize, of course, that you aren't going to tell me what you're afraid was in the letter that may have gone to one of your neighbours and told them something about you that you don't want me to know, so suppose we stick to murder for the moment. When there's been a death in the family, you can generally reckon there's a noticeable gap left behind. A lot of people will be aware of the fact that someone has dropped out of sight. They may have gone to the funeral themselves if it was all legitimate and aboveboard, or they may simply have seen a few lines about it in the deaths column of *The Times*, or they may just have heard about it by chance, in which case they can't be absolutely certain that it's happened. Well, have there been any unconfirmed deaths among your neighbours?"

The two sisters exchanged looks, then shook their heads.

"No deaths," Constance said.

"Disappearances, then," Andrew suggested.

"Disappearances, yes," she answered.

"Go on and tell me about them."

She gave a rueful smile. "The extraordinary thing is how many people have disappeared. It hadn't occurred to me till we started counting them up yesterday, thinking along the same lines as you, but when we did count them up we were really astonished."

"Yes, astonished," Mollie said. "One person after another and all of them seeming perfectly natural, except—except perhaps one."

"Start with that one, then," Andrew said.

"No, I think we'll save him up for the end," Constance replied. "Let's begin with the Eckersalls. It happened first, for one thing, about three months ago. They're two sisters, Jean and Kate, both in their sixties, I should say, and they live in that thatched cottage you may remember we passed in the car before we turned in here where the dog was in the gateway, barking at us. They're crazy about dogs. And they're crazy about gardening. They've a beautiful garden. You hardly ever pass it without seeing one or other of them at work in it. They're very good neighbours. If one's got a touch of flu they'll always go shopping for one, and they bring one bulbs and seedlings for the garden, and they invite one in for enormous teas, where all the cakes are homemade and so good that if you aren't accustomed to having tea at all, as I'm not, you're completely put off eating anything else that day."

"And which of them has disappeared?" Andrew asked.

"Oh, neither of them," Constance answered. "It was their old father who vanished one day."

"He must have been at least eighty-five," Mollie said, "but according to what Jean told me one day, he suddenly took it into his head to go out to Australia to stay with his son Kenneth, who went out years ago and I think has a fruit farm near Adelaide. He's been home once or twice, but not for some time now, and the old man made up his mind, Jean said, that he wanted to see him once more before he died. So off he went and naturally we didn't give it a second thought till yesterday, when Connie and I began to wonder—well, we haven't exactly been wondering, because of course that would be absurd if you knew Jean and Kate. All the same, we put him down on our list of people who've disappeared."

"What's he like?" Andrew asked. "Are they fond of him?"

"He's a possessive, domineering, selfish old bastard," Constance replied. "If he'd been my father I'd have been delighted to see him go off to the Antipodes and shouldn't have grieved much if he hadn't survived the journey."

"Oh, come, Connie," Mollie protested. "He wasn't as bad as all that."

"As bad or worse," Constance said. "But people like that, if only they're ruthless enough and insensitive enough, have a way of getting away with everything they want. I honestly believe his daughters, poor souls, are devoted to him."

"Do they ever talk about his coming back?"

The sisters looked uncertainly at one another. Constance frowned.

"I can't say I remember their ever having done so," she said. "But Mollie knows them much better than I do. Have they ever talked about it to you, Mollie?"

"I remember Jean saying they were going to redecorate his bedroom for him before he came back," Mollie said, "but that was some time ago and she didn't say anything about when it was likely to be. I got an impression he might be away for a fairly long time."

"So that's our first possible victim," Andrew said. "Unpleasant bully of an old father, murdered by two daughters who couldn't take it any longer. Who's next?"

Mollie gave an uneasy little titter. "It sounds dreadful, putting it like that," she said. "It makes it all sound quite unreal."

"That may be a good reason for doing it. Go on."

"Well, there's Mike Wakeham," Constance said.

"Who's he?"

"The Wakehams are our next-door neighbours. They're young and good-looking and I think moderately prosperous and they hate one another."

"That sounds more promising," Andrew said. "And he's vanished, has he?"

"Please," Mollie interrupted, "you mustn't take too much notice of what Connie says about people. She pretends to be much more censorious than she really is. She doesn't mean half of it."

Andrew was inclined to believe that she meant most of it. He had never thought of Constance as exactly an intolerant woman, but only as someone who from time to time enjoyed sharpening her wits at the expense of other people, and who certainly did not suffer fools gladly.

"He's got rather a habit of vanishing," she said. "He's done it at least twice before, to my knowledge, and when he does it, Naomi, his wife, has a way of coming to see Mollie and weeping on her shoulder and saying she can't stand it anymore, she's simply got to divorce him. But it always ends with her taking him back."

"Are there any children?"

"No."

"So that isn't the reason she sticks to him. You're sure it's because of women that he vanishes, are you?"

"It seems likely, doesn't it, unless now and then he finds he's simply got to have a rest off Naomi. She's a very intense blonde who can't get over the fact that she gave up a wonderful career on the stage to marry him. The career tends to get more wonderful as time goes on."

"What does he do?"

"I'm not sure. He's something in the City. I've an idea he's in a firm of stockbrokers, but I'm not sure about it. Naomi drives him into Maddingleigh in the morning and he takes the train to London, and she picks him up again in the evening. Then about three weeks ago he simply didn't come back and he hasn't been seen since."

"And his wife has no trace of him?"

"Not so far as we know."

"Do you know if she's reported it to the police?"

"Oh, she wouldn't do that!" Mollie exclaimed. "If he's simply gone off for a short time with another woman, she wouldn't want to bring them in on it, would she? I mean, think of the humiliation. I don't believe she's told anyone about it but Connie and me and perhaps one or two other friends."

In fact, a gossip, Andrew thought.

"What do his employers think about it?" he asked. "Hasn't she been in touch with them?"

The sisters exchanged looks again, then shook their heads.

"We don't know," Constance said. "After all, there are certain things one doesn't ask a person even when they're pouring their heart out to you. Or seem to be pouring out their heart. As a matter of fact, there's a complication in the present situation which has made us rather careful of what we say to her. We've a suspicion that Naomi's got an affair of her own going at the moment, and that that might even be the reason why Mike's stayed away. We may be quite wrong about it, but in a place like this that sort of thing gets around, and it's a fact that Nicholas Ryan is spending an unusual amount of time in the old house and a good deal of that time with Naomi."

"Ryan," Andrew said thoughtfully. "Why does that name sound familiar?"

"You've probably heard it from us," Constance answered. "It was old Mrs. Ryan whom Mollie worked for for all those years and who left her so much money. Well earned, one may say, but still, it was generous of her. Nicholas is her grand-nephew and all she left him is that Victorian monstrosity down the lane. It'll bring in a very handsome sum if he ever succeeds in selling it, but I don't think he's finding it easy to get rid of. Unless someone wants to turn it into an old people's home, or something like that, it may be very hard to sell. It's too big and inconvenient and ugly. Still, he doesn't seem to hold it against Mollie that his old aunt left most of her money to her. He's an easygoing, friendly young man with a casual sort of attitude towards money and possessions generally. I'm not sure what he does for a living. Sometimes I wonder if he's on the dole and just camps in the old house now and then when it suits him. But of course he may have inherited plenty of money from some other relative. Anyway, every time he talks to us about what he's doing, it's something different. I know he's been a courier for a travel firm, and he's worked in a company that was making some kind of very modern furniture, and in some kind of project—I think it was voluntary—which was sending food to starving Africans. And that may mean he has money of his own. I always find it very refreshing to talk to him, because you never know what may be coming next. And besides that, he's very good-looking."

"And definitely isn't one of the people who's disappeared," Andrew said.

"No, as I told you," Constance said, "he's around the place rather more than usual."

"Then are Mr. Eckersall and Mr. Wakeham the only ones who've really vanished?"

"Well, as a matter of fact, no," she said.

"Go on then, who are the others?"

There was a slight pause, then Mollie asked, "Do you think a woman counts?"

He was puzzled. "The murder of a woman is generally thought to be as important as that of a man. I don't think there's ever been any inequality in the matter."

"No, but what I mean is—" She hesitated, weaving her fingers together and looking as if she did not know how to set about explaining something. "In that letter that came to me, you see, it says, 'Don't forget I saw you bury *him*...' That means the dead person, if there really is one, is a man, doesn't it? So the fact that our doctor's wife left him two or three weeks ago isn't— What's the word I want?" She looked helplessly at Constance.

"Relevant," Constance said.

Mollie nodded vigorously. "That's it. Relevant. The letter can't have had anything to do with that, can it?"

"It doesn't sound like it," Andrew agreed. "All the same, tell me about it."

"We don't know much about it," Mollie said, "but David Pegler's been my doctor for years. And he looked after Mrs. Ryan too. He lives in that nice Georgian house at the crossroads. His practice is mainly in Maddingleigh, but he and a partner hold a surgery twice a week in Clareham, and we used to see quite a lot of his wife, Carolyn. She's a good deal younger than he is. I suppose he's about fifty and she's only thirty-five, but I always thought it was a happy marriage. And then one day apparently she just left him. He isn't the kind of man who tells you much about himself and all he said to me in a sad sort of way was that she'd gone and he didn't suppose she'd be coming back, and I remember I gave him a cup of coffee and we went on and talked about cricket. He's secretary of the village cricket club and tremendously keen on it. He really keeps the club going. And I suppose Carolyn went off with some other man she'd fallen desperately in love with, or something like that, but I really don't know anything about it."

"And that's the lot?" Andrew asked.

"No," Constance said again.

"I was just thinking it wasn't a very promising bunch," Andrew said, "but you've been keeping something up your sleeve, haven't you?"

"We did say there was one disappearance that didn't seem altogether natural, didn't we?" She reached for the coffeepot and refilled their cups. "Actually I find it very hard to talk about it, even if it's got nothing to do with the letter, or with murder, because it's still a real tragedy. There's a young couple who live across the road in the cottage next to the Eckersalls'. Their name's Gleeson. Jim is Leslie's second husband. He's a quantity surveyor, working in Maddingleigh. And they've a son—they had—that's to say, Leslie had or has—oh dear, I'm afraid I'm getting confused. What I'm trying to say is that Colin, who's about eleven, if he's still alive, is Leslie's son by her first husband, who I believe was killed in a car crash, so Jim is Colin's stepfather, and the relationship between the two of them has never been good. Jim's a difficult sort of man, very touchy and suspicious, and Colin's a very self-assertive sort of child. But I don't know what he did to make Jim lose his head one day, because usually you could see he tried very hard to hold himself in when Colin was getting on his nerves. But something happened and Jim gave Colin a real beating up and after it Colin ran away and hasn't been heard of since. And Leslie's been absolutely devastated by it. Of course she hasn't forgiven Jim and I don't think he's forgiven himself, yet it seems to comfort them in some way to cling to one another, rather as if they feel they're both guilty for what happened. But if that letter has anything to do with Colin..."

"Yes?" Andrew said as she paused.

She drank some coffee and did not reply. A cloud had settled on her face.

There was a little silence, then Andrew said, "Presumably the police were brought in on this."

"Oh yes, immediately!" Mollie broke in with a kind of eagerness, which seemed to have been brought on by her sister's reluctance to say any more. "They've been here, asking endless questions, and every few days they come to the Gleesons and say they think they've found Colin, and then it turns out to have been a mistake and it makes poor Leslie feel worse than ever. I think she and Jim are really sure Colin's dead. But of course it's the not knowing that's so terrible for them. I believe every time their telephone rings they expect news of some sort, and then it's nothing."

"How long ago did this happen?" Andrew asked.

"About a month ago," Mollie answered.

"Well, you know what the story makes me feel," Andrew said. "It seems to me there's no question that Constance should take that letter to the police. If the child's dead, whether he was killed by Gleeson or some chance passerby who picked him up when he was trying to run away, they ought to know that there's someone hereabouts who saw it happen, or at least saw the body being disposed of. Constance, you know you've no choice about it, whatever secret of your own you may be afraid may come to light. You've got to go to the police."

"No!" She stood up abruptly. "Now let's go for a walk. Let's forget I ever told you anything about the letter."

Chapter Two

Andrew was acquainted with that flat "No!" of Constance's. He had encountered it a number of times in days gone by, and he had learnt that the best way to deal with it was simply to retreat. Argument achieved nothing. It only led to her digging her heels in more and more firmly. In any case, he was not an argumentative man. Conflict upset him, and he had learnt that if he quietly left the room, leaving Constance for the time being in possession of the field, it was probable that she would presently follow him, having apparently forgotten that they had ever argued about anything and being ready to concede whatever he wished. So he said now that he would very much like to go for a walk and said nothing more about the letter.

Mollie did not accompany them. She wanted, she said, to get the spare room ready for Andrew. Starting out, Constance and Andrew turned to the right in the lane, passing first a small house very like Mollie's, and then Lindleham House, the mansion in which she had looked after Mrs. Ryan for fifteen years.

It was a massive, graceless house, built of the liver-coloured brick that never weathers and with facings the colour of dried mustard. It had a couple of small turrets sprouting out of the slate roof, a pretentious porch and rows of tall, blank-looking windows. If heavy curtains had not been visible at them, the house would have looked uninhabited.

The garden obviously had once been a fine one, but it appeared to have been neglected for some time. There was a soft blue haze of speedwells in the grass, which had not been mown for a long time, a charming sight really, and if only speedwells had been difficult to grow, lawns such as these might have been treasured. But unfortunately they sprouted all too easily, like the splendid dandelions, the delicate cow parsley and the white-flowered nettles that choked the borders. If Nicholas Ryan wanted to sell the house, Andrew thought, it would be to his advantage to lose no time in employing a gardener.

He and Constance walked slowly, with Andrew reducing the length of his stride to match hers. Her back was still straight and her air was brisk, yet there was the stiffness of age in her movements. For a little while they hardly talked, but presently they began to chat about the mechanism of the absorption of sucrose into the cell, a subject in which they had both been interested in the past, and a sense that this was a normal thing to be doing when he and Constance were together and that anything else that they had talked about that day was a kind of fantasy, came to Andrew and made him feel that it was very pleasant to be here among the soft hawthorn scents of the countryside on such a kindly May day. Instead of believing that they ought to be discussing the anonymous letter and that there was something craven about having abandoned his insistence that it be shown to the police, he began to hope that the matter need not be raised again.

Not that he thought for a moment that it would not be. Give Constance a little time and she would return to it herself. She had come to him that morning for advice and sooner or later she would probably ask for it.

However, for the rest of the day the subject was avoided. When they returned from their walk Andrew found that a room had been made ready for him and, retiring to it, he unpacked the

small suitcase that he had brought. As he did so he found words
beginning to pound in his brain.

> *Then up spake brave Horatius,*
> *The Captain of the Gate...*

Catching sight of his own face in the mirror as this
happened, he scowled at it. He could not have been less interested than he was in what brave Horatius had had to say, so
why could the man not leave him alone? And if this reciting of
verse to himself whenever his mind happened to be empty, or
was resisting the intrusion into it of thoughts that he wanted
to avoid, was so firmly built into his makeup that he could not
escape from it, why did the verse always have to be the sort of
thing that he had admired when he was ten years old? Why
could it not be perhaps a little Shakespeare, or some Donne
or Milton, poets whom he had discovered when he was a little
more mature? Just occasionally it was, but today Macaulay went
relentlessly on.

> *Then up spake brave Horatius,*
> *The Captain of the Gate,*
> *"To every man upon this earth*
> *Death cometh soon or late..."*

An indisputable fact. Trite, in fact. But unfortunately
it raised in Andrew's mind once more the dark question of
whether or not death had come sooner than it ought to one of
the people about whom he had been hearing earlier in the day.
The old man who had gone to visit a son in Australia. The man
who had an odd habit of leaving his wife without warning or
explanation. The doctor's wife, who, however, was probably safe
and well because she happened to be female. The little boy who
hated his stepfather.

Was one of them dead and buried probably somewhere
near, and was it Andrew's duty to find out the truth about it?

It was next morning that he heard more of the story of one of the people who had disappeared, though not from either Constance or Mollie. They had spent a quiet evening watching a Chekhov play that happened to be on television, then they had all gone to bed early. It had surprised him a little to find that although Mollie was the more generally domesticated of the sisters, it was Constance who did most of the cooking. But it was not really surprising that, as in everything else at which she worked, she should turn out to be extremely competent. Dinner had been a simple meal consisting of a soup that had certainly not come out of a tin, lamb cutlets, courgettes and new potatoes, and then a fresh fruit salad, but everything had been perfect. Breakfast, however, Constance left to Mollie, and though Andrew was faced with a fried egg, a sausage and bacon, to which he was not accustomed, Constance herself drank only black coffee.

After it, Andrew walked out into the garden. The spell of fine weather was lasting and sunshine lay warm and glittering on the lawn at the back of the house, on the beds where the rose bushes were putting out their new shoots and where wallflowers and forget-me-nots bloomed together in the borders. A wooden fence against which a clematis had been trained divided the garden from that of the house next door. There was a bench under an old walnut tree at the bottom of the lawn, and after walking up and down for a little while, he sat down on it and tried to think lucidly about the situation into which he had got himself.

He had a feeling that Constance would not be sorry if he were to say that he had to return to London that day. She had gone to him in a panic, wanting his help, but by now, he thought, she was more afraid of his questions than she was of handling the situation by herself. Perhaps his questions had helped her to clarify her view of the problem, but he realized that it had become even clearer to her than it had been at first that she did not want him probing into what she feared had been in the letter to Mollie that might have gone astray.

What Mollie was thinking at the moment he was not so sure. She was the kind of woman who would always feel happiest if she had a man to advise her, even if in the end she would not dream of taking his advice. Of the two sisters he could easily imagine her being the more stubborn, because she was the less rational. But what did she want? Did she really hope that he could solve some mystery for her?

He did not know how long he had been sitting there when a voice startled him.

"Good morning. You must be Professor Basnett."

Looking round, he saw a woman regarding him over the fence that divided the sisters' garden from that of the Wakehams. All he could see of the woman was her head. It looked as if it was balanced without any neck on a clump of clematis. She had very fair hair, which fell softly around a narrow, pointed face with large dark eyes and a small but full-lipped mouth. Supposing that this was Naomi Wakeham, Andrew remembered that Constance had described her as an intense blonde, and even with only her head showing above the fence, he thought that he could recognize a questioning intensity in the way that those surprisingly dark eyes regarded him.

He stood up and went towards her.

"Good morning," he said. "Are you Mrs. Wakeham?"

"Yes," she said. "Mollie told me that you were probably coming down to stay. Are you busy at the moment?"

"I'm doing nothing at all."

"Then would you care to come round for a cup of coffee?"

Andrew was not sure which he felt more, curiosity or alarm. Curiosity because this woman's husband was one of the missing people, alarm because this might be the beginning of finding himself drawn helplessly into the vortex of other people's problems.

"Thank you," he said, "it's very nice of you, but—"

"Oh, do come," she interrupted. "I've just been making some coffee for myself. And as a matter of fact, there's something I rather specially want to ask you."

That set the alarm bells ringing, yet curiosity won.

"Well, if I may just tell Constance and Mollie where I've gone—"

"Oh, don't bother about that," she said. "I saw Constance drive off to the shops a few minutes ago and Mollie's always busy about the house at this time of day, so just come round, and as it's such a lovely morning, I'll bring the coffee out into the garden. Come straightaway. I'm so glad to have a chance to talk to you."

She disappeared abruptly, which made Andrew think that to talk to him over the fence she must have been standing on something which raised her high enough to be able to look over it.

Going out of Mollie's gate and turning in at the Wakehams', he saw that this was in fact so. Evidently she had been standing on a wooden bench against the fence. It had a rough wooden table in front of it and two garden chairs near it. But Naomi Wakeham herself had disappeared.

However, she emerged from the house almost immediately, carrying a tray with cups, a plate of biscuits and a coffeepot on it. She was a tall, slender woman of about thirty whose fair hair fell in soft loops on her shoulders and whose fine skin was tanned a faint golden brown. She was wearing a loose green-and-white-striped shirt, green jeans and sandals, and looked elegant in a carefully casual way.

She put the tray down on the table.

"Of course you'll have guessed it," she said. "Mollie told me you'd once been involved in solving a murder, and I thought—" She stopped abruptly. "Do sit down. How do you like your coffee? Cream? Sugar?"

Andrew sat down in one of the garden chairs. He saw that the garden was very like the one next door, except that it looked more neglected. But this woman's husband, he remembered, was one of the people who had disappeared, and perhaps she herself was not a keen gardener.

"Black, please, and no sugar," he answered.

She sat down on the bench. Her movements were lithe and graceful.

"But is it true?" she asked.

"That I once helped solve a murder?" he said. "I suppose you could say so."

"And do you know a great deal about crime?"

She had poured out coffee for them both, had put her elbows on the table and was resting her chin on her hands. Her gaze was fixed on his face, intently searching.

He felt foolish and began to wish he had not come.

"Virtually nothing," he said. "I'm a retired plant physiologist and for some years now I've been writing the life of Robert Hooke."

"Who's he?"

"He was a natural philosopher in the seventeenth century. He was an architect too. In those days people weren't forced into narrow specialization as they are today. But he's particularly celebrated for pioneering microscopical work in a variety of fields and was the first microscopist to observe individual cells."

It was not very kind of him, but he hoped to deflect her from her present line of inquiry by the simple method of boring her.

He failed. She merely waited till he paused, then said, "I'd like to tell you about my husband. You see, for all I know, he's dead. Even murdered. I don't really think so, but he might be. And I don't want to tell the police about it because if he came back and found I'd done that, he'd be furious. And when he's furious he gets violent and I get frightened. But I've simply got to talk to somebody, so you don't mind if I tell you all about it, do you? You see, it's much easier to talk to a stranger than to someone one knows. It's almost like talking—well, to a doctor."

Andrew recognized the symptoms of someone who revelled in dramatizing herself and decided not to take it too seriously.

"Why not try it out on your doctor, then?" he suggested.

"On poor little Pegler? Oh God, he'd only hold my hand and sympathize. Besides, his wife has just walked out on him, as

Mike has on me, so I doubt if he's in a fit state to bother about anyone else's emotional problems. No, what I need from some kind person is detachment—detachment, wisdom, experience. So you do understand why I've turned to you, don't you, after everything Mollie's told me about you?"

"Mollie doesn't really know me very well," Andrew said defensively. "It's Constance who's my old friend."

She looked faintly contemptuous. "She's a very brilliant person, I'm sure, but she's all intellect, she doesn't know anything about *people*."

"As a matter of fact, she knows a great deal about people," Andrew said.

She shook her head. "Not really. I expect she can be clever about them and tell you what their neuroses are and that sort of thing, but she doesn't really feel for them. Mollie's different. She's got a warm, intuitive sympathy with one when one's in trouble. She seems to know what one's going through without one's having to explain it all. But perhaps, after all, I shouldn't be talking to you like this. It's embarrassing you. Let's talk about something else. How long are you staying here?"

"A day or two. I'm not sure."

"And you've known Constance a long time?"

"Oh yes, for years."

"But you've never been here before, have you?"

"No, she and I usually meet in London."

"Why haven't you married her?"

He thought that he was beginning to understand her. Besides enjoying dramatizing herself, it pleased her to be deliberately outrageous. He decided not to spoil her pleasure.

"At our age it hardly seems necessary," he said.

"You've been married, though, haven't you?"

"Yes."

"Did your wife leave you?"

"No, she died."

"Oh dear, I'm sorry. I'm sorry, I'm sorry, I really am. You mustn't take any notice of the way I talk. I've no tact. I never have had. I've a bad habit of saying whatever comes into my head. Was it long ago?"

"About ten years."

"My husband left me three weeks ago and I'm still reeling from the shock. I feel as if I'll never get over it. He didn't even pack a suitcase, you know, though I think he had some money. I drove him to the station in Maddingleigh, as I usually did, and that's the last I've seen of him. And someone at the firm he works for in the City rang up a day or so later and asked me what had happened to him, was he ill or what, and I improvised and said he'd got pneumonia and had had to go into hospital. And they've rung up once or twice since then and I've elaborated the story a little, but I shan't be able to keep it up indefinitely and he'll be sacked and I'll be left without any money. I'm going nearly distracted with worry."

"You were on the stage once, weren't you?" Andrew said. "Perhaps you'd enjoy going back to it instead of relying on such an undependable person."

An unexpectedly shrewd look came into her big, dark eyes.

"So Constance and Mollie have been talking about me," she said. "What frightful gossips people are, even one's best friends. I suppose they told you Mike had gone off with a woman."

"That seems to be their theory," he admitted.

"It's what I've let everyone think," she said. "Of course it isn't true."

He raised his eyebrows in a questioning way, but held back from asking her what she meant. She would hurry on quickly enough, he thought, if he was silent.

He was right, for after waiting a moment for him to express surprise, or at least interest, she said with a touch of defiance, "It's never been a woman. He's disappeared once or twice before, though never for as long as this, and if it had been because of a woman, I should have known. I know him so well, you see. If he'd been away with a woman he'd have come home shivering with guilt, probably bringing me an expensive present and begging me to forgive him and swearing he'd never do such a thing again. But it was never like that at all. Each time he vanished he just took a taxi home from Maddingleigh one day, walked in here as if he'd just come back from the City as usual, seemed glad to see me, kissed me and asked what there was for dinner. Then he asked whom I'd told about his having been away and I said, 'Just Mollie,' and he said, 'Good girl,' and told me that if ever he disappeared again I was never to tell anyone about it, least of all the police. D'you know what I think?"

Andrew expressed regret that he did not do so.

"I don't believe in that job of his in the City," she said. "I believe he's working for MI5, or 6, or one of that lot. And when he disappears, it's because he's been sent away to do some special job. Don't you think that must be it?"

An acute desire came to Andrew to say that he had a pressing appointment elsewhere and to get up swiftly and go. He had come to Lindleham to try to help Constance to make sense of an anonymous letter, not to get dragged into a spy thriller. But he had always been a courteous man and knew that he could not leave in that way.

"Suppose you're right," he said, "why should those supposed employers of his keep ringing you up to ask what's happened to him? They must know all about what he's doing."

Her face went sombre. For a moment he thought that she was going to burst into tears. Then he remembered that she was an actress and decided not to let himself feel too moved.

Giving a deep sigh, she answered, "Of course, that's one of the reasons I'm so worried. If they really don't know where he is, then it can only be because something's gone wrong and he's been murdered, or kidnapped by the Russians, or something. I tell you, it all keeps going round and round in my head till I don't know where I am. I'm fond of him, you see. Not exactly in love with him anymore, because he's such an aloof sort of person who doesn't really want one to care for him, and he has an awful temper if he doesn't get what he wants, but we got on all right in a sort of way, so I miss him as well as being frightened about the future. And there's one other possibility that scares me almost more than my idea that he might be working for Intelligence. Because, after all, there's something rather fine about that, isn't there? I mean, it could mean he's working for his country. But this other idea..." She thrust back the fair hair that fell around her face and for a moment stared broodingly before her. "Suppose he's some kind of crook," she said. "Suppose he's been involved with a gang of drug smugglers or something like that all this time. I can imagine it. There's a very violent side to him, besides his secretiveness, and I've never thought he had much moral sense. So suppose he got across someone in the gang and they killed him, and those telephone calls were just to find out if I'd gone to the police about it yet."

"Why don't you do that?"

Never before in Andrew's life had he spent so much effort in trying to persuade people to go to the police.

"But I told you, he said I mustn't," she said. "If he comes back and finds I've done it, he'll never forgive me."

It would be interesting, Andrew reflected, to discover what, behind the screen of fantasy, she really believed had happened to her husband. Probably, he surmised, that he had gone off with a woman. That might be the explanation of his disappearance that she actually found hardest to face.

But it would not be impossible now, he thought, to thank her for the coffee, express the hope that she would soon have some cheering news of her husband and get up and leave.

He was just about to do so when he heard the squeak of the garden gate and saw a young man advancing towards them across the lawn.

He was a very good-looking young man, not very tall, but wide-shouldered and narrow-hipped, with dark hair, dark eyes, wide-spaced above high cheekbones and slightly hollow cheeks. There was something just sufficiently odd about those slanting cheekbones and the slope of the jaw from the broad temples to the sharp chin to save it from being uninteresting. He was wearing narrow grey trousers and a black pullover.

"Nicholas!" Naomi exclaimed, not rising to meet him but tilting her head so that he could kiss her cheek. "I thought you'd gone back to London. You haven't met Professor Basnett, have you? Professor, this is Nicholas Ryan, the nephew of the old lady Mollie used to look after, and who owns the hideous mansion next door."

An idea that seemed to come out of nowhere suddenly slid into Andrew's mind. A moment after he had spoken he wished that he had not, but by then it was too late.

"Is that the house that's for sale?" he asked.

The young man sat down on the bench beside Naomi. It was not unattractive, Andrew thought, that his ears were a little pointed. When he was older, when there were wrinkles in his smooth olive skin and he had begun to stoop a little, there would be something intriguingly gnome-like about him.

"Don't tell me you're interested in it," he said with a disbelieving grin.

"Well, I've got a certain idea at the back of my mind," Andrew said, "which perhaps isn't very realistic, but if I just happened to find the right house, I think I might begin to consider it more carefully. It happens, you see, that at my age one's got to start thinking about the future. One isn't always going to be fully mobile. One's going to need help of all sorts. And so I've been looking around recently at some of those developments for old people where you can get a bungalow or a flat with a certain amount of service, and where there's a tolerable restaurant. You know the sort of thing I mean." Once they had started, the lies flowed surprisingly easily. "But there's generally a serious snag. To get into any of the better places you have to go on a waiting list, and for some of them you even have to go on a waiting list to get on the waiting list. So I've begun to wonder if I might not create my own small-scale old people's development. If I could find the right house..."

"You're thinking you might buy a big house and convert it and sell or rent it out in flats?" Nicholas Ryan said. He looked impressed, but was there a glint of mockery in his eyes? "And of course install a housekeeper. You know, if you were serious about this, you couldn't do better than employ my Mrs. Grainger. She was my aunt's cook for years and she's been looking after the house for me ever since my aunt died. She's a wonderful woman. But perhaps that's going ahead rather fast. You aren't really serious about this, are you?"

"I'm not sure," Andrew replied. "As I was saying, if I found the right house, I might go ahead with it. Getting it all organized would give me an interest in life, for one thing."

"I thought you were interested in that man Hooke you were telling me about," Naomi said.

"Yes, but this would be something new. Designing the flats, working out what the needs of a group of old people really are, going into the financial side of it all—oh, I think it might be well worth undertaking."

Why was he doing this? he wondered. Why did he feel an urge to probe into the lives of these two people? For that, of course, was what he was doing and he knew that it was just what Constance would have wished him to do. She had brought him down here simply to assess the characters of her friends and neighbours, to find out if he felt that any of them was capable of committing the murder of which the anonymous letter had accused Mollie. But he would much have preferred, or at least he believed that he would have preferred, to keep clear of the whole matter. So why was he actually looking for trouble?

"If you're serious," Nicholas Ryan said, "I could take you round straightaway and show you over the place. But you'll find it's ugly, inconvenient and even a bit damp. There's no central heating and only one bathroom in that whole huge pile. The two lavatories, one for the family and one for the servants, were originally earth closets, modernized about fifty years ago, with good, solid wooden seats. And even on a lovely day like this there's a queer chill in the place. Some of the rooms never seem to get warm."

"It doesn't sound as if you're trying very hard to sell it," Andrew said.

"Well, to a friend of Naomi's I'd tell the truth," the young man replied. "Apart from that, I'm telling you nothing you won't see at a glance. But would you like me to show you over it?"

"Now, do you mean? Would that be convenient?"

"If you'd like me to do that, yes."

"Then if Mrs. Wakeham will excuse us..." Andrew stood up. He found that Naomi was looking at him with a slightly puzzled frown.

"Remember," she said, "everything I told you was in confidence."

"Of course," he said.

He thanked her for the coffee, and he and Nicholas Ryan walked towards the gate.

The gates of Lindleham House were open and in the lane outside them was a blue Mini. As Andrew and his companion turned in at them and started walking up the weed-grown drive towards the house, a woman emerged from it and came briskly towards them. She was in the blue uniform of a district nurse, with a neat little blue hat on her short grey hair. She looked about forty and was small, plump and rosy-cheeked, with plain, blunt features in a round, freckled face and grey eyes that looked strangely enlarged behind a pair of thick, round spectacles.

She gave them a good-humoured smile and said, "Good morning, Mr. Ryan."

"Good morning, Nurse," he answered. "Been in to see Mrs. Grainger?"

"Yes, I've just given her her injection," she said. "Poor woman, I'm shockingly late, but we had to cope with an emergency this morning. I suppose you don't mean to stay here, do you?"

"For good, do you mean?" he asked. "Good Lord, no."

"I was just thinking that if you were, you could learn to give her the injections. That would save me some trouble. I know she'll never learn to do it herself. The mere thought of doing it seems to make her come over queer. Some people are like that about injections. Oh well, never mind. We always have a nice chat when I come. I've just been having coffee with her. Bye-bye, Mr. Ryan."

"Goodbye, Nurse. Thank you for coming."

She trotted on down the drive, climbed into the Mini and drove away.

"You see, Mrs. Grainger is diabetic," Nicholas Ryan explained. "And she's past the stage of being able to treat it with diet or tablets. Still as strong as a horse in her way, but actually it makes it a little difficult for her to find a job and why it suits her to stay on here and look after a house that's generally empty. A woman comes in from Clareham to help her clean, but otherwise she does everything. And that's very lucky for me, living in London most of the time as I do, as she's so wonderfully reliable and efficient. As I told you, she was with my aunt for years and of course knew your friend Mollie Baird very well and is very attached to her. But I suppose it wasn't a very good idea recommending her to you for the sort of thing you have in mind. It's just that I don't like the idea of her being turned out of a place where she's been for so long. But she may be looking for an old people's home herself some time soon. Now come in and have a drink, then I'll show you round."

He pushed open the massive door in the Gothic-looking porch, which was unlocked, and led Andrew into a large, square hall. It had a high ceiling, ornamented with plaster fruits and flowers, a floor of slippery-looking cream-coloured tiles and a wide staircase covered in an aged Turkey carpet. A plump cupid, very decently draped, held up a lamp at the bottom of the stairs. As Nicholas Ryan had warned Andrew, it struck him at once that there was a disagreeable chill in the place.

"Come in here," Nicholas said, opening a door. "It's not as morgue-like as the other rooms."

It was a smallish room, which Andrew thought had once been somebody's study or office. It had one tall window with dark-green velvet curtains framing it, a mahogany desk against one wall, a remarkably small iron grate in the middle of an ornate marble mantelpiece, two leather-covered armchairs and a bookcase filled with heavy volumes of what looked like a very old-fashioned encyclopaedia. It was sombre and far from welcoming, but at least sunshine was pouring in at the window and there was a tray with bottles and glasses on the desk.

Nicholas went to the desk, asked Andrew what he would have and when he asked for whisky and soda poured out a considerably stronger one than any to which Andrew was accustomed. He did the same for himself.

"And now," he said, indicating to Andrew that he should sit down in one of the armchairs and taking the other himself, "tell me why you really wanted to come here, because you aren't thinking of opening any old people's home, are you? And you aren't interested in the house. Who could be? So what do you really want?"

As he spoke the flicker of mockery had returned to his eyes.

"I'm as transparent as that, am I?" Andrew said. He sipped some whisky.

"You weren't totally convincing, anyway," Nicholas answered. "I wondered if perhaps it was just that you wanted to get away from Naomi. It's odd how she affects some people. Of course I'm very fond of her myself, but I've an odd sort of mind, you see. I find those fantasies of hers really entertaining. I keep wondering what she'll come up with next. What was it today? That Mike's left her for the Himalayas to go into a Buddhist monastery, or that he's sailing a boat single-handed round the world?"

"She did say it was confidential," Andrew answered cautiously.

Nicholas laughed. "Then shall I guess what it was? It's that he's an agent for MI5. Wasn't that it?"

"She did seem to suspect something of the sort."

"Or perhaps it's that he belongs to a gang of crooks in London who've probably murdered him. But don't get her wrong. She's a dear girl who'll do absolutely anything for anyone who's in trouble. When the Gleeson kid disappeared—I'm sure you've heard about that—and Leslie Gleeson's been nearly round the bend ever since, Naomi's been splendid. Of course, she rather enjoys playing the sympathetic friend. All the same, I sometimes think if it hadn't been for her, Leslie might have killed Jim because of what he'd done to Colin, and then probably she'd have killed herself as well. Still, that wasn't why you actually wanted to come round here, was it? So what was it? A pressing desire for my company?"

Andrew decided to go as near to the truth as he could.

"As a matter of fact, you aren't so very far wrong," he said. "I was hearing about you yesterday from Constance and Mollie and I thought it might be interesting to know you better. I'm always interested, and I admit to some degree suspicious, when I hear about people who are said to be indifferent to money. So very few people are."

"So that's what they said about me, is it?"

"More or less."

"It's completely untrue, of course. I was almost unbearably disappointed when I heard Aunt Hilda had left nearly all her money to Mollie. But I've never held it against Mollie herself, if that's what's worrying you. And I never thought of contesting the will, or anything like that. Mollie isn't worrying that I still might try to do that, is she?"

Andrew gave a slight, ambiguous shrug of his shoulders.

"It was a perfectly good will and quite reasonable in the circumstances," Nicholas said. "Mollie had lived with my aunt for fifteen years and they'd been close friends. She looked after her devotedly when she became almost helpless after having a stroke and she deserved all she got. There was never any question of undue influence. And the will was witnessed by David Pegler—he was my aunt's doctor—and Lorna Grace, the district nurse you've just met, both of whom are very respectable citizens."

"But it wasn't drawn up by a solicitor?"

"No, I don't believe it was. But it was all perfectly legal, though as a matter of fact there was a question... But there was nothing in that." Nicholas frowned slightly as he looked at Andrew inquiringly. "I suppose Mollie isn't suffering from a bad conscience about it all? I mean, about having inherited so much when all I've got is this white elephant of a house. She's the kind of person who might think that was unfair. But if that's what you were sent round here to investigate—I mean, to find out what my feelings are about the whole matter and do I think she cheated me—you can tell her to forget it. I've a reasonable income inherited from my father, who was a quite successful surgeon and I'm able to live in idleness. Perhaps it would be better for me if I couldn't, but that's how it is. And I've been told that sooner or later I ought to get a couple of hundred thousand for the house. And I was never a particularly good nephew to my aunt. I'd sometimes let two or three years pass without coming to see her, and then I'd only stay for a day or two. We weren't very fond of one another. It's true I somehow always took for granted that she'd leave me her money because of the habit one tends to have of thinking that money will stay in the family. But really I rather admire Aunt Hilda for disregarding that sort of nonsense. She left what she had to the person she cared for most."

"Are you doing anything now?" Andrew asked, remembering what Constance had told him of how this young man drifted from one thing to another.

"Nothing at all," Nicholas said. "As I told you, I've enough of my own to get by on. I've a quite pleasant flat in Fulham and from time to time I try my hand at a little freelance journalism, but the cheques I get for it are rather few and far between. Luckily, that doesn't matter to me."

"What was the question about the will that you just mentioned?"

"Oh, that. A muddle of some sort. According to Pegler and Lorna Grace, who were coming in to see my aunt almost every day at that time, they witnessed two wills, about a month apart. But they didn't know what was in either of them, and the second will, if there really was one, was never found. Mrs. Grainger seemed to be the only person who perhaps knew something about it. Incidentally, in the will that was proved, she was left quite a generous legacy. Anyway, she claimed that my aunt, who was half paralyzed and couldn't do much for herself, managed to tear up some papers about three days before she died and asked her to get rid of them. And when we came to look for the second will, the only one we found was the one that was made a month before. So I think my aunt just changed her mind at the last moment and destroyed the thing, because, you see, the only other person who could have destroyed it was Mollie, and I find it hard to see her doing that. Not impossible, perhaps, but hard, don't you think so?"

Andrew nodded thoughtfully. A very disturbing idea had just occurred to him, but he did his best to keep his face expressionless.

"Of course, I could have destroyed the thing myself," Nicholas went on, "because I was here on the spot. I was paying Aunt Hilda one of my rare visits when she took it into her head to make this new will. Actually I didn't even know she'd done it. Pegler and Lorna Grace said nothing about it at the time. But if I'd known, and no one can prove I didn't, and I'd found that I wasn't even going to be left this magnificent mansion, I might have burnt the thing to make sure I got something. Or I might have burnt the wrong will by mistake. That's a possibility you might consider. If the second will left me far more than the first, and I thought I was burning the first when in fact I'd got hold of the second, it might be all my own fault. Not very likely, somehow, but such things can happen."

He spoke with detachment, as if it were not of himself that he was talking.

Andrew stood up.

"I've taken up enough of your time," he said. "Thanks for the drink."

"And have you got what you came for?" Nicholas asked.

Andrew met the young man's smile with a smile of his own.

"I'm not sure," he answered truthfully. "About Mrs. Wakeham..."

"Yes?"

"If her stories about her husband's disappearance are all fantasies, as you suggest, hasn't he got very tolerant employers? The truth about them is said to be that they're a firm of stock-brokers, isn't it? And she claims that she's put them off by saying Wakeham's in hospital. But if that was the case, wouldn't they have expected him to send a medical certificate or something? You don't think by any chance..." He hesitated.

"Well?" Nicholas said.

"Oh, that one at least of those fantasies is the truth. I mean that he's working for people who know quite well where he is.

"MI5, indeed!" Nicholas laughed. "My own belief, if you want to know what it is, is that he isn't working for anyone at all. I believe he was sacked some time ago when he first decided to go off for some time on his own, and he's only been putting on a show of having a job in London while in fact he's been fairly frantically trying to find another. And I think Naomi knows it and that's why she's so desperately worried about money. Because that at least I think is true. She's really worried. But whether or not she knows where Mike is I haven't the faintest idea. I wouldn't be surprised if he's just been lucky enough to find a rich woman to keep him. He may be living luxuriously in the South of France, or some such place, by now."

He stood up and opened the door for Andrew.

"I believe Mollie and Constance are old friends of yours," he said.

"Yes," Andrew replied.

"You're someone they'd turn to if they were in trouble of any kind."

"Perhaps. What kind of trouble had you in mind?"

"Nothing special. Anyway, now you can reassure Mollie, can't you, that I don't harbour any resentment against her because she inherited what I thought was coming to me? I was a fool to think I could rely on family feeling without working at it and I deserved what I got."

"How long are you staying here?" Andrew asked.

"I'm not sure. A week or two. I want to stir up the house agents in Maddingleigh about this house and see to a few things. I'm sorry you didn't really want to buy it."

He saw Andrew to the front door. As he started down the drive he was aware that the young man remained in the doorway for some time, looking after him.

A number of thoughts were churning round in Andrew's mind, and if in themselves they were disturbing, they at least had the merit of keeping brave Horatius at bay. He had not given a thought to him all that morning.

All the same, Andrew did not like the idea which Nicholas had indirectly suggested to him that Mollie might be the person who had disposed of Hilda Ryan's second will. Yet she could have been. In the first place, she had been on the spot and could easily have done it. Also she had benefitted greatly by the first will and might perhaps have done far less well by the second. Nicholas Ryan had visited his grandaunt just before her death and perhaps had been at his most attractive and affectionate and had roused in her the feeling that after all he was her only living relative and that money should be kept in the family. Besides that, Andrew felt fairly sure that Nicholas himself believed that Mollie had destroyed the will.

But if he did, then there could be two reasons for his doing so. One of them was simply that she had had both motive and opportunity. The other was far more complicated. It was that Nicholas was the person who had received the letter that had been meant for Mollie, a letter that threatened to expose her for having destroyed the will and so confirmed his already existing suspicions that she had done this. But if that was so, then it almost certainly meant another important thing. It meant that the letter that Mollie had received, accusing her of murder, had been intended for Nicholas Ryan. And that probably meant that Andrew had spent the morning drinking and chatting with a murderer. A very charming one, but nevertheless, a murderer.

Chapter Three

But if Nicholas Ryan was a murderer, the next question was: whom had he murdered?

Mike Wakeham, because Nicholas was in love with his wife? He had not spoken of her as if he was in love with her.

An old man who was said to have gone to Athustralia? Why should Nicholas have done that? To oblige the old man's daughters, who had not had quite the nerve to do the deed themselves? It seemed unlikely.

The wife of Dr. Pegler? But as the letter had referred to a male corpse being buried, she seemed to be out of it.

An eleven-year-old boy? Why do people kill children? A lot of people do it for all sorts of reasons, most of them peculiarly horrible. But did Nicholas Ryan seem to be the sort of person who would feel impelled to commit the more perverse sort of crime? He gave the impression of being fairly normal. But what murderer is normal? So who could tell?

Suddenly it occurred to Andrew that even if Nicholas seemed to know what might have been in the letter that ought to have gone to Mollie, it did not necessarily mean that he was a murderer. It might be simply that he had written it himself. He might be the blackmailer.

A remaining question that Andrew asked himself as he walked back to Mollie's house was how much of all these matters that were going through his mind he should discuss with Constance. Sooner or later he would of course have to do this, but should he do it now?

A chance saved him from having to make up his mind about this immediately, for as he turned in at the gate he saw that someone had arrived at the house just before him and was now hammering on the door with the knocker.

It was a young woman, probably in her late twenties, slim, red-haired, very pale and very distraught. She might have been good-looking if her eyelids had not been swollen by recent tears and her face set in a grimace of misery. She was in the uniform of the day, soiled jeans and a loose shirt. She did not seem to be aware of Andrew walking up the path after her.

The door was opened after a moment by Mollie.

The girl threw herself into her arms, hid her face against Mollie's shoulder and burst into more tears.

"It's happened again, Mollie," she sobbed. "Again! I can't bear it, Mollie, truly I can't bear it!"

Mollie drew her into the house. At the same time, having seen Andrew standing on the path behind the girl, she gave him a little signal with her head that he should come in too. He followed them in and closed the door behind him.

Mollie took the girl into the sitting room. Andrew, unsure whether or not to leave them alone together, lingered in the hall, but Constance, emerging from the kitchen, touched him on the arm, nodding towards the sitting room, and the two of them went together into the room.

Mollie and the girl had sat down side by side on the sofa.

"Tell me about it, Leslie," Mollie said.

"The police came, just as they've done before," the girl said. "They said—they said they thought they'd found him.

They wanted Jim and me to go and identify him. And, oh God, Mollie, it was so horrible. The poor little boy."

"But it wasn't Colin."

"No."

"Leslie, this is our friend Professor Basnett, who's staying with us," Mollie said. "Andrew, this is Leslie Gleeson, whose little boy has vanished. You remember, we told you about it. Leslie dear, would you like a drink? Perhaps some brandy. I think you ought to have something."

Leslie Gleeson gulped, gave Andrew a watery stare, mopped her face with a sodden handkerchief and muttered, "Thank you."

Constance saw to the pouring out of a glass of brandy for the girl and brought it to her. She also poured out whisky for Andrew and sherry for Mollie and herself.

"Go on, tell us what happened," Mollie said. "The police wanted you to identify a dead child, was that it?"

"Yes, they came this morning and told me—oh, they were very nice about it, they tried to be as gentle as they could, I realized that, but still, it was so terrible." Leslie swallowed some of her brandy as if she was not aware of what she was doing and gave a shudder as the alcohol went through her. She went on: "They said they'd found the child over in the river beyond Maddingleigh. They didn't know how long he'd been there. His body was caught under the roots of a tree and might have been there two or three weeks anyway. And he was about Colin's age, they said, and had fair hair like his, but they couldn't tell anything by his clothes because he was naked, and—oh, Mollie, they didn't exactly tell me so, but I realized they meant he'd been raped, and when we saw him we could tell he'd been battered horribly. His nose and one of his arms were broken. And they said he'd been held under the water and drowned. The utter wickedness of it! How is it possible to do things like that to a little boy? I know one's always hearing of horrors like that on television, but one doesn't think one's going to have to see it for oneself."

"But it wasn't Colin," Mollie said, her arm still round the girl.

"No, but you see, it could have been. Something just like that could have happened to him. And I believe it has. Now that I've seen what it can be like, I believe it has. I'm sure he's dead and perhaps awful things were done to him first. If he isn't dead, where is he? It's a month since he disappeared and they've shown his picture on television and all, but no one's come forward to say they've had a glimpse of him. So I'm sure he's dead. But if the police want me to look at another body after what I saw today, I don't think—oh, I know I'll go, because it might be Colin—but I don't know how I'm going to bear it."

"You mustn't give up hope yet," Mollie said. "He's a clever child, you know. He may just be playing some kind of trick on you in revenge for the beating Jim gave him and he's hiding somewhere. Then he'll get tired of it one day and come home again."

Andrew did not know if she believed a word of it. A month was a long time for a child of eleven to be wandering the world on his own. But the words seemed to have at least a temporarily calming effect on Leslie Gleeson. Drawing a little away from Mollie, she mopped her eyes with sudden fierceness as if she held them to blame for her tears, then thrust her handkerchief into a pocket of her jeans and drank some more brandy.

"Perhaps you're right," she said in a husky but controlled voice. "As you say, he's clever. Perhaps he's persuaded someone to look after him. Squatters or people like that, who wouldn't ask too many questions. Yes, I'm sure you're right. That's what's happened. Now I wanted to ask you, and you too, Constance, and of course Processor Basnett, if you'd come round to us this evening for a drink. It would be a help if you would. Jim and I—well, we hardly speak to one another nowadays, you know. We don't quarrel or anything, but we just sit silent. In its way it's rather frightening because it isn't what Jim used to be like. And after this morning I know it'll be worse than ever. So if you'd come round and just try to chat about ordinary things and make Jim join in, I'd be so grateful. It won't be much fun, of course, but I know you understand. Will you come?"

"Of course, dear," Mollie said.

"About six o'clock." The girl stood up. "I'll be seeing you then, Professor Basnett. I'm sorry I made such a scene the first time we met. I don't know what you think of me. But I'll be more sensible this evening. Goodbye."

Mollie saw her to the door.

After she had gone Constance asked Andrew, "Where have you been all the morning?"

"I had coffee with Naomi Wakeham," he answered, "then a drink with Nicholas Ryan."

"And what did you make of the two of them?"

By then Andrew had made up his mind that for the present he was going to say very little about what had passed through his mind that morning concerning Nicholas and Naomi, not to mention Mollie. But after a moment he said, "I didn't have long with either of them. Only long enough to come to the conclusion that Naomi isn't in the least worried about her husband's disappearance because she can spend her time happily in a world of fantasy in which he's either an agent for MI5 or a member of a gang of drug smugglers. And that's much better than having a mere stockbroker around the house. And Nicholas—well, he's a subtle character. I should say that he's shrewd and that he might be devious and ruthless. On the other hand, he might be a quite generous and kindly young man. I didn't make up my mind about him. But I was doing what I thought you wanted me to do, taking a quick look at your neighbours to see if any of them strikes me as a probable murderer. Now what about my giving one of my piercing glances at the two Miss Eckersalls? Is their father down under in Australia, or simply down under the earth?"

"I think that could be arranged," Constance said. "In fact, we could go round this afternoon. They've promised us some seedlings for the garden and I could say we've come round to collect them."

It was about three o'clock when Constance took Andrew across the lane to visit the Eckersall sisters. Before they went she told him a little about them.

"There was a time when I thought their brother Kenneth and Mollie were going to get married," she said. "He was here on a visit and he wanted it, but Mollie had settled in by then with Mrs. Ryan and she told me she thought it was too late to think of starting a new life on the other side of the world, leaving all her friends behind. But he still writes to her sometimes and sends her a Christmas card every year. It was sad in a way, I thought at the time, that she wouldn't have him, because he was a pleasant sort of man, not exciting, but kindly and reliable and loyal. In fact, the right sort of man for a middle-aged woman to marry. But Mollie seemed to be perfectly happy where she was and wouldn't move. I didn't give her any advice, of course. I was still living in London and we used to see each other only occasionally. Mrs. Ryan used to let me come and stay in her house sometimes and that's how I got to know Kenneth. And his sisters, and Mrs. Ryan, and the Peglers, though David Pegler had only just taken over the practice here. And this house and the Wakehams' hadn't even been built and the Gleesons hadn't arrived yet. Their cottage was in a fairly derelict condition, lived in by a man called Banks who used to work for a scrap-metal dealer in Maddingleigh, with a wife who was usually three parts drunk, and he and his boss got sent to prison because it turned out the scrap they dealt in was mostly stolen. And his wife left Lindleham soon afterwards, and the cottage, which actually belonged to Mrs. Ryan, as she used to own all the property round here, was sold to the Gleesons, who've turned it into a very attractive place."

"What happened to the wife who drank?" Andrew asked.

"I don't know, and I don't know what happened to her husband either after he got out of gaol. I don't think his sentence was a very long one, but they never came back here or to Clareham. I don't even know if they stayed together. Now let's go over to the Eckersalls', shall we? They've been away for some time, I think, walking in the Highlands, but I saw them in their garden this morning, so I know they're back."

She fetched a trug from a garden shed behind the house in which to bring back the seedlings that she and Mollie had been promised, and set off with Andrew to the cottage on the other side of the lane.

The same brown dog that had barked at them from the gateway when they had arrived the day before was there now and barked at them wildly as they approached it. He was a medium-sized dog of indeterminate breed and appeared to be ready at all costs to resist any attempt on their part to enter the garden. But when they showed that this was just what they intended to do he seemed to decide that his real duty was to make them welcome, wagged his tail and sniffed at Andrew's trousers, then trotted beside him as they went up the path to the door.

The cottage was a low white building with a few dark beams showing in its walls, small windows and a thatched roof. It had a large garden with apple trees in it, bright with blossom, rhododendrons coming into bloom with forget-me-nots covering the ground around them and borders of bushy shrubs. It was the kind of tangled-looking but basically orderly garden which only the skillful gardener can achieve. The front door of the cottage was painted white with a black wrought-iron knocker on it. Constance used it to announce their arrival.

The door was opened by a short, sturdily built woman of about sixty with short, thick grey hair that stood up almost straight from her forehead, grey eyes, a square, deeply tanned face which was strongly lined with wrinkles and a wide, smiling mouth. She was wearing a brown smock-like garment that billowed loosely around her, no stockings, but a pair of emerald-green ankle socks and earth-caked canvas shoes. Constance introduced her to Andrew as Miss Jean Eckersall.

She gave him a firm handshake, as strong as a man's.

"And you've come for the plants we promised you, haven't you?" she said to Constance. "They're just ready. We'll go and collect them." Then she turned in the small, low-ceilinged hall and suddenly bellowed, "Kate!"

A faint voice called back from above, "Hallo!"

"It's Constance and a friend, come to collect some plants," Jean Eckersall shouted. Her voice was vibrant.

"I'll be with you in a minute."

Heavy footsteps pounded across the ceiling overhead, then a woman appeared on the steep, very narrow staircase that curved upwards at the end of the little hall. Except that she was even shorter than her sister, looked perhaps two years older and wore cherry-red socks instead of bright green ones, it would have been hard to tell them apart. When Constance introduced her to Andrew she gave him the same kind of firm handclasp as her sister's.

Jean went on: "We've been meaning to bring the plants over to you ourselves, but we've only just got back from Scotland. Been walking in Sutherland. Marvellous. Most beautiful scenery in the world. And surprisingly good weather, though cold, of course. Such fine people too. We got talking to an old man who seemed just to have his croft and a little bit of land with a few sheep on it and a collie, and he asked us where we came from and we told him from Berkshire and he said, 'I mind those parts well, I was there in 1914.' We felt as if somehow we'd slipped back at least a generation, but the next thing he was asking us was what we thought about the Economic Community, and he knew much more about it than we did. And he'd this dog he was thinking of putting down because he's got his collie and didn't need a second one, and this fellow's such a mongrel, poor darling, he wasn't worth anything. So we bought him for next to nothing and brought him home." She bent and stroked the dog that had followed Constance and Andrew into the cottage. "You're a darling, aren't you, eh?" she said to it lovingly. "Not as handsome as our poor little Timmie, but we're going to be very, very fond of you."

"What happened to Timmie?" Constance asked. "Did you board him in a kennel somewhere while you were away?"

"You mean you didn't hear?" Jean Eckersall said. "I thought everybody knew. No, that horrible child, Colin, killed him."

"Colin Gleeson?"

"Yes, of course. Oh, a dreadful child. I know he's disappeared and his poor mother's frantic and all that sort of thing, and it's all very tragic. But really he was a quite horrible child. Perhaps not his own fault, perhaps just a bad bringing up, but I don't really believe that. I think some people are born with that sort of cruelty inside them."

"But what did he actually do?" Constance asked. "How did he kill Timmie?"

"With a catapult. Come along, we'll show you where it happened."

The sisters led the way through a door beside the staircase that opened into the garden. There was a lawn there that sloped downwards to a beech wood, and like the gardens on the other side of the lane, it was divided from that of the cottage next door by a high wooden fence. Clematis, roses, ivy and jasmine grew against the fence, and at one point there was a fine old chestnut, smothered just now in clusters of pale blossom. When he first saw it Andrew thought that it was growing in the sisters' garden; then he realized that it actually stood in the garden next door and that only its branches hung over the fence.

"You see," Jean said, pointing up into the tree, "that awful child used to climb up into the tree and come over to our side and take potshots at birds and the squirrels that sometimes come up from the wood, and sometimes at Timmie. We told him again and again that he mustn't do it, but actually he wasn't a very good shot and we didn't worry too much, though we told him we'd tell his parents if he went on. And then one day he hit Timmie with a great stone right on the side of his head. We saw it happen. And Timmie just lay down and died." Her voice trembled for a moment. "And we both went straight round to the Gleesons and told them what had happened and that's when Jim Gleeson gave Colin the beating that made him run away. And I know that's terrible, but, well, what he did was terrible too, wasn't it? I mean to our poor little Timmie, whom we both adored. I'm sure he meant as much as a child to us."

"And that's why we went off to the Highlands," Kate said, speaking for the first time, though in the same ringing voice as her sister. Andrew thought that perhaps they were in the habit of conversing with one another from one end of the garden to the other. "We couldn't stand it here. It felt so empty. And we couldn't bear the thought of just buying a new puppy, because that seemed so callous. But when we happened to come across this dear fellow up in Sutherland and heard he was going to be put down, it felt quite different, making an offer for him. And bless him, he's taken to us both and we just love him. His name's Mac, because we felt he ought to have a Scots name."

At hearing his name spoken, the dog gave a responsive wag of his tail.

While the sisters had been talking Andrew had noticed what seemed to him a curious thing. Under the shadow cast by the chestnut tree, there were four mounds in a row, each of them about four feet long and a foot wide, like small graves. Three of them were covered in neatly mown grass and each had a small, carved headstone. On the farthest was the name Mamie, on the next to it Hans, and on the third Spot. The fourth grave, if graves were what they were, and a smooth area around it, could only recently have been covered with squares of turf, for these had not yet joined together, though they had been carefully laid in place, and there was no headstone.

Jean Eckersall saw Andrew looking at it.

"Yes, that's Timmie's grave," she said. "This is our little cemetery. Some people think it's absurd, but why shouldn't dogs who've meant so much to one be properly buried and commemorated? We buried Timmie before we went away, but we only put the turf over his poor little grave yesterday and we haven't ordered the headstone yet. But we'll do it as soon as we can. He was a Yorkshire terrier, you know, quite small, but oh, so intelligent. And Spot was a fox terrier. He was killed in the lane by a car. I was quite sorry for the man who did it. He brought him in to us in his arms and was almost in tears. I don't think it was his fault. Spot was never very good about traffic. And Hans was a dachshund who hadn't been properly inoculated for distemper and who caught it and died. And Mamie was a Labrador bitch who died of old age. We loved her so much that when she died we thought we'd never have another dog, but a friend left Hans with us when she went on holiday, then asked us if we'd care to keep him, and by then, of course, we were in love with him, so it felt almost as if it had been meant. That's how it's been with all our dogs. It's as if each one had some special claim on us. Now let's see about those seedlings. We were going to give you some antirrhinums, weren't we, and some African marigolds and some chrysanthemums? Come along."

She led the way to where some bedding plants had been neatly pricked out in rows. Her sister had brought a trowel, and Constance's trug was soon generously filled.

On the way home she said to Andrew, "Whenever I see the Eckersalls' garden I feel that ours is hopelessly suburban, but neither Mollie nor I are very enthusiastic gardeners. What do you make of our neighbours?"

"Batty in an amiable sort of way," he said. "Or am I wrong?"

"Wrong about them being batty, d'you mean, or about them being amiable?"

"Well, speaking as one who's only a very moderate sort of animal lover, I couldn't help feeling that the death of their Timmie meant far more to them than the probable abduction and murder of Colin Gleeson, and on the whole I think that the murder of a human being does matter rather more than the admittedly shocking murder of a Yorkshire terrier. So I'm not as much in sympathy as perhaps I should be. About their being batty, they aren't crazy enough to have taken revenge on the child for what he did, are they? I mean, that last grave is Timmie's, is it, not Colin's?"

"Andrew!" Constance exclaimed faintly, and gave him a strange, frightened look. He had never seen an expression like it on her face before. "You aren't serious about that, are you?"

"The thought hadn't occurred to you?"

"No!"

"You see, ever since you came to me yesterday with your mysterious letter I've had murder on my mind," he said, "and I find I'm tending to see bodies everywhere. Not, I admit, till today, the body of a Yorkshire terrier, though it's the only creature we're quite sure is definitely dead. But it's somehow confused my thinking. You don't by any chance think, Constance, that that letter was a rather macabre sort of joke, written by someone who saw those women burying Timmie?"

They had reached Cherry Tree Cottage and gone into the sitting room. From its window they could see Mollie weeding a rose bed.

"I don't understand," Constance said. "What could be funny about that?"

"Well, some people have a rather black idea of humour," Andrew replied, "and the Eckersall sisters do rather lay themselves open to ridicule. Of course, whoever wrote the letter couldn't seriously have expected to get any money out of them."

Constance gave a little shudder.

"Then what about the letter that ought to have gone into the envelope that was addressed to Mollie?" she asked. "Was that a joke too?"

"Perhaps."

"And it went to the Eckersalls? Do you really think so?"

"Well, no, I don't."

"Then what do you think?"

"How can I think anything till you tell me what you're afraid is in that letter, Constance? I've an idea what it may have been, and I've an idea who may have got it, but how can I help you if you won't trust me? By the way, about that child, Colin..."

"Yes?"

"Was he as awful as the Eckersall sisters suggested?"

"I think he was a bit of a devil," Constance said. "But I don't know much about children. I daresay he would have grown out of it."

"You don't think he may have stirred murderous hatred in anyone besides the Eckersalls?"

"There was his stepfather, I suppose. They certainly didn't love each other. I think Colin was rather good friends with Naomi Wakeham. And I think he and Nicholas got on pretty well. In fact, I think it was Nicholas who taught him how to use a catapult. Who else in the neighbourhood he may have infuriated I don't know." She gave Andrew a curious look. "Are you seriously thinking someone could have buried him in the dog's grave while Kate and Jean were in Sutherland?"

"It's a possibility, isn't it?"

"And someone else saw it being done?"

"Yes, it could have been seen from the lane. I checked that."

"And then he wrote a letter that got to Mollie by mistake? Don't you think it's far more probable that Colin was picked up by someone in a car, taken away, perhaps sexually assaulted, perhaps tortured and murdered, and then his body dumped somewhere, like that poor child Leslie told us about this morning?"

"Actually I do."

"For some reason that seems to me far worse than that he should simply have been killed by someone in a plain fury," Constance said. "That might even have been done unintentionally. Yet the end result's the same. Death. There's only the degree of suffering he might have undergone while it was happening." She had sat down in a chair near the empty fireplace. She had her elbows on her knees and had taken her head in her hands. Small, neat and restrained, at the moment she looked more vulnerable than usual. "I know I ought to tell you what I think was in the letter really meant for Mollie, Andrew."

"I think I know," he answered.

"About her?"

"Yes."

"How did you find out?"

"I guessed it after the talk I had with Nicholas this morning. But did she really destroy Mrs. Ryan's second will? It's my impression it's what he believes."

"I'm afraid she did."

"Has she actually told you she did?"

She hesitated, then nodded sombrely.

"After she'd done it, she completely lost her head," she said. "She wanted to go straight to the police and tell them what she'd done. And perhaps that would have been the best thing to do. It was I who stopped her. You see, the will cut her out completely except for a legacy of a few thousand. And Mrs. Grainger too. And that seemed so unfair. Both of them had worked for the old woman for years, looking after her devotedly, and she'd made this earlier will, leaving Mrs. Grainger a good legacy and the rest of her money to Mollie, and just the house to Nicholas. I believe it rather amused her at the time to leave him the house, because of the sort of things he used to say about it. She was a rather malicious old thing. But then he came down to see her and spent a few days here, using all his charm on her, and she suddenly made up her mind that everything ought to go to her only relative, and she scribbled a new will and got David Pegler and Miss Grace to witness it, and only three days later she died. I didn't believe she'd been in her right mind when she did it, but David swore she was, and so when Mollie told me what she'd done and I was really scared on her account, I told her to keep quiet about it. And she's inherited the money which I think is rightfully hers. But I'm afraid someone may know what she did and is trying to blackmail her, though I don't see how they can prove anything."

"Was any question ever raised about Mrs. Ryan's death?" Andrew asked. "If that second will hadn't been destroyed, you could say she died at a very convenient time for Nicholas."

She shook her head. "It was a second stroke. David signed the death certificate without any hesitation."

"And he and Miss Grace and Nicholas and Mrs. Grainger and Mollie all knew about the existence of that second will?"

"Yes."

"So if you're right about what that missing letter contained, any one of them except for Mollie could be your blackmailer."

"I suppose so, yes."

"What sort of man is Pegler?"

"A very ordinary sort of man," she answered. "Yes, very ordinary."

Yet all of a sudden her eyes avoided his and she sounded doubtful. Andrew began to wonder if the local doctor might not be as ordinary as all that.

Andrew had an opportunity to form his own opinion about this that evening, for when he, Constance and Mollie arrived at the Gleesons' cottage at about six o'clock they found Dr. Pegler already in the Gleesons' sitting room with a glass of gin and tonic in his hand.

He was a short, plump man of about fifty, dressed in a neat, dark suit, appropriate for his visits to patients. He had a round face under which a double chin had already begun to form folds, a forehead from which the brown hair had receded far enough to make it seem unusually high, grey eyes that looked tired and somehow bewildered and a small mouth which produced a hesitant smile when he greeted the other visitors.

A shy man, Andrew thought, very unsure of himself, and though conscientious, probably not very competent. If Andrew had been his patient, he would not have had much confidence in him. A bored man too. It did not appear to interest him to meet Constance or Mollie or Andrew. He looked as if he would have liked to gulp his gin in a hurry and leave them.

But perhaps that was only normal in someone whose wife only recently had suddenly left him. If he could still carry on at all with his work it was to his credit, and if a merely social evening was rather more than he could bear, it was hardly surprising.

Jim Gleeson greeted his visitors with an air of casual indifference which made Andrew feel that Leslie's idea of having her friends in for drinks had been unfortunate. He gave the impression of being as anxious for them to leave as David Pegler was to get away. Plainly, it was not going to be a particularly pleasant evening. Jim Gleeson poured out drinks for them all in a way that managed to suggest that one drink was all that they need expect and that he would be obliged if they did not take too long over it.

He was a big man of about forty, wide-shouldered and heavily built, wearing an open-necked shirt and cotton trousers. He had heavy, rather coarse yet in some way handsome features. His hair was thick and dark and he had thick dark eyebrows ruled almost straight across his face, above oddly staring dark eyes. A somewhat brutal face, Andrew thought, and wondered just what the boy Colin had suffered at the man's hands before running away. Granted that killing a dog with a catapult was not the sort of thing to be encouraged, it was easy to imagine that punishment by a man of this sort might possibly go too far.

Leslie had changed out of the shirt and jeans that she had worn in the morning into a straight white sleeveless dress with several ropes of beads round her neck. She had brushed her red hair sleekly back from her face and was wearing long earrings of some brightly coloured enamel. The signs of tears had faded from her face, or else had been covered up round her eyes by a thick layer of greenish makeup. She was making an effort to look cheerful, as if the last thing on her mind was that at any moment the telephone might ring and dire news of calamity be sprung upon her.

The room was a small one with a low beamed ceiling. Almost the whole of one wall was taken up by a great open fireplace in which at present a big bowl of lilac stood. A glass door led out into the garden. There was rather too much furniture in the room, as if the Gleesons had moved there from a larger house, but it was extremely tidy and there was a faint aroma of furniture polish in the air, which made Andrew think that Leslie must have whiled away an empty afternoon sprucing the room up to be ready for her guests.

"I saw the Eckersalls in their garden this morning," Leslie said when they had all been supplied with drinks and had sat down. "Home from Sutherland with a new dog. Not a very beautiful fellow, I'm afraid, but friendly once he got tired of barking at me."

"It doesn't seem to take long to get over the death of a dog," Gleeson said. "Why don't we all have dogs instead of children?"

Pegler gave him a swift, reproving look, while Leslie pretended not to have heard what her husband had said.

"Carolyn and I used to talk sometimes about having a pet of some kind," the doctor said. He spoke in a hasty, nervous way, as if once he had got started he was afraid that he might be interrupted. "But we never agreed about what to have. She wanted a dog, but I'm a cat person. Cats always take to me. It's lucky now we didn't get either, as most of the time there'd be no one at home to take care of it. I've been thinking lately of acquiring an aquarium with some of those beautifully coloured fish with long, floating tails in it. Come from Hawaii or somewhere like that, don't they? It would be something more alive than television to have in the house and they'd look after themselves when I have to be out for hours. I'm considering it seriously."

Andrew felt some admiration for the plump little man. Although it was obviously an effort for him, he had plainly decided that the subject of his wife and of her leaving him was not to be taboo.

He went on, still hurriedly: "I heard from her yesterday, you know. It felt rather strange. We talked on the telephone for quite a while and I found it difficult to remember she wasn't just on a visit to friends, or shopping in London, or something, and that she wouldn't be coming home in a few days' time. She asked me how I was and had I got over the cold I'd had when she went away. But actually she'd rung up to discuss a divorce. I told her I didn't know much about the divorce law nowadays. I don't believe either party has to be what they used to call guilty. But I said she should go to a solicitor and get advice and I'd agree to anything she wanted. And I must admit, from my own point of view, the sooner she does it, the better. I don't like loose ends." He emptied his glass and stood up. "Thank you for the drink, Leslie—that was nice. You must come and have drinks with me some day soon when I've got myself sorted out a bit better than I am at present. But I've got to get along to a committee meeting of the cricket club now. We're discussing the new pavilion. We've had some quite generous donations towards it. I've had to write a lot of acknowledgements. Goodbye, Mollie. Goodbye, Constance. Nice to have met you, Professor. No, Jim, don't bother to see me out. I know my way."

Moving with a bouncing sort of speed, the doctor shot out of the door.

As they heard his car drive away, Leslie said, "He's really awfully brave about Carolyn leaving him, isn't he?"

"If he's the kind of man who thinks that fish with floating tails are a good substitute for a woman, I don't blame her as much as I did," her husband said.

"That was only a joke," she retorted.

"But she must have had a good reason for going," he went on. "And he's never said a word about there being another man in the case. It may be he's not as satisfactory to live with as you'd suppose."

"If there is another man, David probably wouldn't say so," she said. "He'd feel we'd think he meant it to her discredit and he's much too nice for that."

"Actually I never took much to Carolyn," Gleeson said. "She seemed to me an ambitious bitch who thought when they married that David was going to make it in the medical world in a way there was never any hope of his doing. Life in a country village, with David wrapped up in his patients and his cricket club, bored her stiff. And if that was so, the best thing for her to do was to get out without hanging around any longer. It'll give David a chance to get married again."

"He talked more about her than I've ever heard him do before," Mollie said. "D'you think that was because of her telephone call? Perhaps it made him think she might come back to him."

"I've a photograph of the two of them that she gave me some time last year," Leslie said. "It was taken after the match when he made his century against Little Millpen." She opened a drawer in a bureau and took out a photograph album. "Look, here it is. Don't they look happy together?"

She handed the open album to Mollie.

She looked at it, smiled, then handed it on to Constance, who only glanced at it, then handed it to Andrew. He looked at the photograph with interest. It showed the doctor in the white trousers and pullover that are still the uniform for cricket, and wearing a pair of dark glasses, but not the helmet and mask that have become normal wear for professional cricketers. Little Millpen's bowling was perhaps not very ferocious. He looked relaxed and cheerful, but it was at the woman who stood beside him with her arm through his that Andrew looked the more thoughtfully.

She was taller than he was and wide-shouldered for a woman, with narrow hips and long legs in black jeans. Her short-cut brown hair clustered around her face in curls. Her features were strongly defined and aquiline. Her attitude to her husband gave the impression of affection and yet of a slightly amused kind of contempt for the pleasure that he was taking in his recent triumph. It was true that the two of them looked happy enough, yet Andrew could easily imagine her being an ambitious woman who found her husband perhaps more than a little ridiculous.

But it was not of this that he spoke when later he, Constance and Mollie returned across the lane to Cherry Tree Cottage. He had been glad when Constance had given the signal for them to leave, for even though Leslie had seemed anxious for them to stay and tried to start a discussion of a serial that was being shown at the time on television, Gleeson had shown no sign of wanting them to stay. He was a hard, ironic man, Andrew thought, determined above all things not to show any sense of guilt at what had happened to his stepson.

"Am I right," Andrew asked as Mollie led the way into the house, "that there was something rather boyish about Mrs. Pegler's appearance?"

"Perhaps there was," Constance said. "Yes. I remember the first time I saw her she was on a bicycle, going shopping in Clareham, and I wasn't actually sure if she was a boy or a girl. It was only when she called out 'Good morning' to me, and her voice was certainly a woman's, that I was certain about it. Why do you ask, Andrew?"

"Isn't it obvious?" he said. "She's one of your vanished ones, who may have been killed by your murderer, but we've been writing her off because of the letter referring to a male, when she's a female. But seen at a slight distance by someone who didn't actually know her and very likely in darkness, mightn't she easily be mistaken for a boy? I think you must add her to your list of possible victims. And that, it seems to me, means that you've got to consider your fish-loving doctor as a possible murderer."

"Don't!" Mollie cried out. "Oh, please, don't!"

"Why, Mollie?" he asked, surprised at her vehemence. "Are you specially fond of him?"

"Yes. No. I mean, I've always liked him," she said. "But tomorrow I've got to go and get my usual pills from him, and if I thought he was a murderer—well, I couldn't take them, I just couldn't!"

Andrew put his arm round her shoulders.

"I'm sorry, Mollie," he said. "Don't take any notice of me. Of course I'm not serious."

She gave him a questioning look, trying to make out if he meant what he said. Andrew did his very best to look as if he had done so.

Chapter Four

Next morning, which was Friday, soon after breakfast Mollie set off to the surgery that Dr. Pegler would be holding in Clareham that day to pick up her pills. She did not take the car, but went on foot. After she had gone Andrew asked Constance what kind of pills they were.

"Just mild tranquilizers," Constance answered. "I don't know if they really do her any good, but she thinks they do, which is the main thing. She started taking them after Mrs. Ryan's death and she's stayed on them ever since."

"And was it because of Mrs. Ryan's death that she needed them, or because of her troubled conscience?"

They had gone to sit on the bench under the old walnut tree at the bottom of the garden. The sky was a clear blue and the sunshine was brilliant. Not a breath of wind stirred the branches over their heads. There was a scent of lilacs in the air.

"Mostly her conscience, I suppose," Constance said unwillingly. "Andrew, you think it was terribly wrong of me, don't you, to have stopped Mollie telling the police what she'd done with the will when she herself wanted to do it?"

"I think it may have been unwise," he said. "I don't like the idea of taking it on myself to say how wrong it was."

"It was wrong. I know now it was wrong." She turned away from him as if she did not want to see in his face how deeply he might be criticizing her. "But I was so angry. As I saw it at the time, that old woman had cheated Mollie. If she'd never said anything about leaving her the money it would have been different, but she'd told her explicitly that except for the legacy to Mrs. Grainger and the house that she was leaving to Nicholas, Mollie was to have everything. It was a promise. So it seemed as if at last, almost for the first time, something was going to go right for her. She's had a terrible life, you know. One thing after the other has gone wrong."

"I don't know much about her life," Andrew said. "You've never talked a great deal about her."

"I suppose I haven't. By the time you and I got to know one another there wasn't much to say except that she was in a mental home for a while, and that wasn't a thing I specially wanted to talk about. It wasn't for long and it wasn't for anything much. She recovered completely. Or it seemed as if she did. When she told me what she'd done with the will I did wonder if perhaps some of the old difficulties lingered on, and that was partly why I didn't want her to tell anyone else what she'd done. I thought it might push her over the edge again. Now I think it would have been the best thing for her to do. Her mind would have been at ease. But I can't say my own conscience has ever troubled me about it. For me it was always a question of what would be best for Mollie."

"You said she'd had a terrible life," Andrew said. "What else went wrong?"

"Well, you see, it began so promisingly. She was such a sweet, affectionate, cheerful child, and you can't think how pretty she was. I might have been jealous of her if she hadn't always been so fond of me. I was just the clever one, and that never seems very important to the young. Mollie was really beautiful. She was our mother's favourite too, though our father always tried to make me feel that he expected great things of me. He was a solicitor and he rather hoped at one time that I'd go in for the law, but science was nearly as good and he always gave me all the help he could and I've had a very good life. I achieved far more than I ever expected. But Mollie obviously was destined for marriage, so she never really got trained for anything. And then, sure enough, when she was only twenty, she married Martin Baird."

Her soft, distinct voice quavered for a moment.

"I'm certain it would have been a very happy marriage, he was such a gentle, understanding boy and desperately in love with Mollie. But then he was killed at Dunkirk. And after that Mollie went into the A.T.S. and after a time she started going out with another man and I believe in the end they would have got married but he was killed in an air raid and Mollie had the first of her breakdowns. She said she brought death to people. Both of our parents were dead by then and there was no one but me to help her. She came and lived with me for a time in London, where I'd got my first job in the university, and financially things weren't too difficult, but I never felt I did as much for her as I ought. And I think perhaps I've felt guilty about that ever since. It may be why I did what I did about the will."

"She didn't go into a mental home then?" Andrew asked. He was thinking how radically wrong his assessment of Mollie had been. He had assumed that of the two sisters she was the practical one, the heartier, the more robust.

"No, by degrees she recovered," Constance said. "The war was over by then and I got her to do a secretarial course and then get a job as a secretary, but she didn't stay in it long and drifted on to helping a friend to run a guesthouse. But that didn't last long either. She never stayed in anything long after she'd had her second breakdown and been in a home for a time, till she got her job with Mrs. Ryan. And I believe that one of the reasons why that worked so well was that Mrs. Ryan was a kind of mother to her. I told you Mollie was our mother's favourite and I think she missed her terribly when she died. She's always needed someone to look after her. And then Kenneth Eckersall appeared on the scene and I thought in the end they might get married, but she wasn't even interested."

"Was your feeling that she needed someone to look after her the reason why you left London and came to live with her here?"

"Partly, I suppose. But it suits me very well too. It isn't any great sacrifice. I don't think I'd ever be unselfish enough to make a big sacrifice for anyone. Mollie might be, but I wouldn't."

He gave her a long look. Her face was still turned away from him, and her sharp profile, it seemed to him, looked older and more strained than usual.

"Constance, are you afraid that Mollie wrote you that mad letter herself?" he asked. "Is that why you really asked me here, to see what I made of her? Is there another breakdown on the way?"

She hesitated for a moment, then turned her head and smiled at him.

"No, Andrew, that wasn't why. It's true when we first got the letter I wondered if Mollie could conceivably have written it to herself, but when we talked it over her behaviour was so entirely normal—I mean, it was a mixture of bewilderment and worry and even a touch of amusement—that I put that out of my mind. And the reason that I've asked you here—well, I suppose it was so that I could do what I've been doing. I wanted to confess to someone I trusted my own part in what was done about Mrs. Ryan's will and ask for advice about what Mollie and I should do now. Then my courage failed me and I decided not to tell you anything about it. And I might not have done it now if you hadn't practically stumbled on the truth yourself, talking to Nicholas. Tell me, do you think he really knows Mollie destroyed the will?"

"I don't think he can claim any actual knowledge of it," Andrew said. "He's got no evidence. It's just that he's fairly sure of it."

"Because it was in the letter meant for Mollie that got to him?"

"Not necessarily. I think he could have guessed it simply from the way the will disappeared. Mollie was the obvious person to have destroyed it. And he told me very explicitly that he didn't mean to contest the earlier one and did it in a way which I felt he almost meant as a message to Mollie not to worry."

"You think he's really so generous?"

"It's possible."

"But if it was in the letter that got mixed up with the one that came to Mollie he may be a murderer."

"Just so."

"But you don't think he is."

"I've no opinion on the matter. But to tell you the truth, I rather took to him."

"Everyone does." She stood up. "But what a lot of time we're wasting, talking about something that anyway was probably just a bit of nonsense. I wonder why Mollie's taking so long. Her pills are usually ready waiting for her at the surgery. She only has to pick them up. I suppose she's gone to have coffee with someone she's met. Would you like some coffee?"

Andrew said that that would be very pleasant and Constance went into the house to make it.

She brought it out presently and they drank it there in the shade of the walnut tree and after a little while found themselves calmly and interestedly discussing the development of buds in a callus culture, which to Andrew was a far more rewarding subject than anonymous letters and murder. It was not until nearly lunchtime that Constance began to show signs of serious worry at Mollie's continued absence.

"It's nearly one o'clock," she said. "I wonder what she's doing. She was going to pick up some things for lunch in the village shop. Not much. Just some eggs for omelets and some fruit. But we've really nothing much else in the house at the moment, so we'll have to wait for her. Let's go in and have a drink."

They went into the house and Constance poured out sherry for them both.

As they sat down she said, "She can't simply have forgotten you're here and need feeding."

"Didn't you say she'd probably met a friend and was having coffee with her?" Andrew said.

"But even if she did that, she'd be home by now."

"Anyway, I'm sure she's all right. What could have gone wrong?"

"Only it isn't like her."

"Perhaps on her way, after the coffee, she met someone else who asked her in for a drink, so she made a second stop."

"Perhaps." But she did not sound convinced. "If she doesn't come in soon, could you survive on bread and cheese? There's some steak in the fridge, but we meant that for this evening."

"Bread and cheese or a sandwich is all I ever have for lunch at home," Andrew assured her.

"All right then, we'll give her a bit longer, then I'll get it." She sipped some sherry. "I expect you're right. She's having a drink somewhere and hasn't noticed the time. All the same, it really isn't like her."

"Perhaps she's been persuaded to stay for lunch by whoever asked her in."

"In that case, she'd have telephoned. Oh, let's not worry about it. She'll be in any time now."

But half an hour later Mollie had not returned and Constance had gone out to the kitchen and had come back with bread and cheese on a tray and with a puzzled frown on her face. By two o'clock the bread and cheese had been eaten and the tray had been cleared away, but Mollie had still not returned. Constance's frown was more bewildered and more worried.

"D'you know what I think I'll do?" she said. "I'll ring up Mrs. Roberts."

"Who's she?" Andrew asked.

"She's David Pegler's receptionist. Of course, the surgery was over long ago and she'll have gone home, but I've got her number and she can probably tell me if Mollie was there this morning, and if—if everything was just as usual."

"How often does she go along for the pills?" Andrew asked.

"Once a month."

"Constance, what is it you're really afraid of?" He looked into her brilliant blue eyes with troubled affection. "Is it the breakdown you've been half expecting?"

"I don't know, I just don't know." Her voice grew almost shrill on a note of protest. With a slight sense of shock he recognized that he had not realized till then how tense she was, how deeply concerned for her sister she must have been for a long time. "But something's wrong and I'm going to telephone Mrs. Roberts and see if she can tell me anything. And would you do something for me, Andrew? Will you listen in on the extension in the dining room? Then you can tell me if you've any ideas about what may have happened. I know I'm not altogether sensible about Mollie. Will you do that?"

"Of course."

He got up and went to the dining room, and when he heard her voice in the sitting room saying that it was Constance Camm speaking, he took up the telephone and listened.

He heard a pleasant woman's voice say, "Oh, good afternoon, Professor Camm. How are you? Such lovely weather we're having, aren't we? I'm sure your garden's looking a treat. I was just going to go out and have a go at the weeds in mine. I've really let them get on top of me this year. It was taking an early holiday that did it. I went to Malta and I had a wonderful time. But then of course I came home and heard the sad news about Dr. Pegler—well, I ought not to talk about it, of course, but you'll know all about it, so I don't suppose it matters. Only I wished I hadn't been away, because perhaps I could have helped. Not that one ever really can, but one would like to think one was there in case there was anything one could do."

"You're talking of Mrs. Pegler leaving her husband, I suppose," Constance said, stemming the flow. "No, I'm sure there was nothing any of us could have done, and for all one knows, it may be for the best. But I just wanted to ask you, Mrs. Roberts, did you happen to see my sister this morning?"

"Mrs. Baird?" the other voice replied. "Oh yes, she was in for the usual pills. Looking very well, I thought. Why? Isn't she at home? I remember she left with Nurse Grace, who happened to be in for a talk with Dr. Pegler. I do like that new hat the district nurses wear now. So much smarter than the old ones. I told Nurse Grace hers suited her beautifully. D'you know, it's years since I've worn a hat and I always used to love having a lot to fit my different moods. But of course, they do squash one's hair flat—"

"Mrs. Roberts, my sister didn't say to you she was going to Maddingleigh or anything like that?" Constance interrupted firmly.

"No, as a matter of fact, we didn't talk much," Mrs. Roberts said. "We'd rather a busy surgery this morning. There was the children's clinic for one thing, when they come in for their inoculations, and Mr. Ryan was in, I remember, and—oh, a real stream of people. Poor Dr. Pegler got terribly behindhand with his appointments and he's looking so tired, I felt quite worried—"

"I suppose you don't remember what time my sister left," Constance interrupted again.

"I couldn't tell you, I'm afraid. I know I kept her waiting for her pills for quite a time because there was such a rush on, but she was chatting to Mr. Ryan and didn't seem to mind, and then, as I said, she left with Nurse Grace. I think Nurse gave her a lift home, because I could see from my window where her car was parked and I saw them both get into it." There was a moment's pause. "You're worried about her, aren't you, dear? She hasn't come home, is that it?"

"Yes."

"Well, I really shouldn't worry, because if she didn't feel well or anything like that you can be sure Nurse would have looked after her. Only you'd think she'd have let you know about it, wouldn't you? Yes, I see it's strange. She's so reliable. Well,

I'm very sorry I can't really help you. All I know is, Mrs. Baird came in as usual and left with Nurse Grace. I think your guess is probably right that she went into Maddingleigh to do some shopping. Perhaps she got offered a lift by someone and didn't have a chance to telephone. I'm going there myself tomorrow, because Crowther's have a sale and I want some shoes—"

"Thank you, Mrs. Roberts, I'm sure you're right. I'm sorry to have troubled you."

"Oh, that's all right, dear."

"Goodbye."

"Goodbye."

Both women put their telephones down.

Andrew replaced the instrument that he was holding and returned to the sitting room. Constance was still standing by the telephone with her hand on it and with a look of grave uncertainty on her face.

"You heard all that?" she said.

"Yes," Andrew answered.

"Of course, I don't believe Mollie went into Maddingleigh. I only said that to have something to say."

"I know. But why not try telephoning Miss Grace now? She could tell you where she put Mollie down."

"Yes, I'll try that." Constance picked up the telephone directory and started flipping over the pages. After a moment she dialled a number. She let it ring for some time before giving up. "No one at home," she said.

"Then try Ryan. We know he talked to Mollie this morning. He may be able to tell you if she said anything about what she meant to do."

Constance nodded, found a number on the pad that lay beside the telephone and was just about to dial when she paused and said, "Will you listen again, Andrew? It'll be easier than reporting the conversation to you."

He went back to the dining room and as before listened in on the conversation that followed.

He heard a man's voice say, "Ryan speaking."

"This is Constance," she said. "Nicholas, did you happen to see Mollie this morning?"

"In the surgery?" he said. "Yes, we chatted for a few minutes. But she isn't ill, is she? She told me she'd just come in to pick up her usual pills. I thought she was looking very well."

"Oh yes, she's quite well," Constance said. "I just wondered—oh dear, I don't know how to say this. But can you remember, did you see her leave?"

There was a pause before he answered, then he said, "What's the trouble, Constance? Something's wrong."

"It's only that she hasn't come home yet and she hasn't telephoned or sent a message or anything to tell us what she's doing, and that isn't like her. I thought of telephoning you because Mrs. Roberts told me you were in the surgery this morning and she saw you and Mollie talking. So I wondered if she'd told you she was thinking of going into Maddingleigh or anything like that."

"No, we talked mostly about my boil. I've an unpleasantly painful boil in a fairly unmentionable place, and I'd gone in to see David to get a shot of penicillin. I left before Mollie. I think she was talking to Jim Gleeson when I left. I believe he hurt his back some time ago and I gathered it's been playing up recently, so he'd taken a day off work to see David and get some dope for the pain. Nasty things, backs. I gather that once you've got that sort of trouble the chances are it'll plague you on and off for the rest of your life. I remember my mother had a bad time with hers. In those days they used to call it lumbago. Now I believe they call it chronic strain, or that's what Jim told me was the trouble with him. But you aren't really worried about Mollie, are you, Constance? To think of the worst that could have happened, I mean if she'd been in an accident, perhaps been knocked down by a car, you'd have heard about it by now from the police."

"Yes, I'm sure you're right." Constance's voice had become crisp, as if she was now in a hurry to put an end to the conversation. "I'm sorry to have bothered you, Nicholas. I hope the boil clears up soon."

Andrew heard her put the telephone down.

He had just put down the one that he was holding and was about to rejoin her when he realized that she had picked up the one in the sitting room again and was dialling once more. Assuming that she would want him to listen in, he picked up the instrument that he had just put down and held it to his ear.

"Leslie?" he heard Constance say. "Is Jim in? Can I speak to him?"

"I'm afraid you've just missed him," Leslie Gleeson answered. "He stayed at home this morning because his back was giving him hell, but a couple of drinks before lunch made him feel better and he's gone in to work after all. He'll be home about six o'clock, I expect. Shall I tell him to call you when he gets in?"

"No, don't bother," Constance said. "I may ring again, but it may not be necessary. I just wanted to ask, was he in the surgery this morning?"

"I think he was. I went into Maddingleigh myself on the bus to Crowther's sale and bought a set of sheets and pillow-cases. Very pretty and a real bargain. But Jim said he was going to see David. There are some pills he gives Jim that help him a good deal. This trouble with his back is quite a recent thing, you know. I do hope it isn't going to go on and on, because for one thing he can't cope with the garden and it's beginning to look an awful mess. He started digging up the wallflowers and was going to plant out some dahlias for the autumn, but it gave him agony. But why do you want to know about his going to the surgery?"

"I just wanted to know if he happened to see Mollie there. It doesn't matter. It isn't important."

All the same, Constance slammed the telephone down with a violent clatter. Her nerves were getting the better of her.

When Andrew returned to the sitting room she was still standing by the telephone as if she was thinking of making yet another call, but then she walked away from it and sat down.

"I'm being stupid about this, aren't I?" she said. "There's no reason to worry."

"I wish I knew," he answered.

"I mean, it isn't as if she was a child who couldn't go missing for more than an hour or two without its meaning that there was probably something wrong."

"The person I'd like to talk to is Miss Grace," Andrew said. "You were given pretty definite information that she and Mollie left the surgery together. I was thinking, if you'd tell me where she lives, I'd go and see if she's got home. And if she hasn't, I might be able to find someone who can tell me when she's likely to be in, or where she probably is now. There might even be someone who saw her with Mollie."

Constance frowned, considering his suggestion. She was gazing down at her hands, which were locked tightly together in her lap. The knuckles were white. Then she looked up at him with a quick little smile and nodded.

"That would be very good of you. Thank you, Andrew."

"Will you come too?"

"Would you mind going alone? I don't think Lorna Grace likes me very much."

"For any special reason?"

"A kind of jealousy, I think. Of my job and my having been fairly successful in it. She resents it in another woman."

"I see. Well, tell me her address and I'll go."

"Shall I drive you to the village, or would you sooner walk?"

"I'd rather like the walk. And don't brood too much while I'm gone, Constance. I know it's because of Mollie's general state of mind that you're so worried. You're afraid she may have done something fairly crazy. On the other hand, she may walk in at any time with some perfectly reasonable explanation of what she's been doing. I know I haven't seen much of her, but she didn't give me the impression of being someone who was on the verge of a breakdown. But just tell me how to find Miss Grace. And don't be too disappointed if I don't find out anything. We can always fall back on the police, you know, if Mollie seems really to have vanished."

He saw her start as if until he mentioned the police she had not been taking her own concern really seriously. Then she opened her handbag, which was on the floor near to the chair where she was sitting, took out a small address book and told him where to find Lorna Grace.

A few minutes later, as Andrew set off along the lane towards the crossroads, he found to his intense annoyance that brave Horatius had taken possession of his mind once more. It churned around in his head.

> *"For how can man die better*
> *Than facing fearful odds,*
> *For the ashes of his fathers,*
> *For the temples of his gods...?"*

The trouble was not that in going to see Nurse Grace he felt that he was facing fearful odds. It was true that he did not look forward to it. She was only too likely, he thought, to consider his anxiety, or rather Constance's anxiety about Mollie's non-appearance, as foolish. Mollie was a grown woman who surely could look after herself. But what had really distressed him and what he was trying to blot out of his mind with a dose of Macaulay was the thought of his own tactlessness in referring to Mollie as possibly having *vanished*.

The moment that he had used the word he had seen the stricken look on Constance's face, and though she had done her best to erase it immediately, it had of course reminded him that one of the reasons why he was in Lindleham was to investigate the strange way in which a number of its inhabitants had vanished. An old man. A young boy. An unfaithful husband. A wife who for whatever reason had also absconded.

How Mollie's failure to return home from the surgery could tie in with any of these he had no idea, but it was plain that Constance thought that it could. Or was he making a mistake by assuming that? Was the reason for her distress something quite different?

She had spoken of Mollie having had two breakdowns, but that was a word that could mean almost anything. It could mean, for instance, that Mollie had had intolerable attacks of depression and had sat and wept for several hours at a time without knowing why and had perhaps even attempted suicide. It could mean that she had suddenly and inexplicably turned against Constance and had gone wandering off by herself, forgetting who she was or where she was going. If that was what had happened Andrew could understand why Constance was so anxious now. But there were all sorts of possibilities. Schizophrenia, for instance. He was not sure exactly what the word meant, but he knew that it was a pretty bad thing and that it would be terrible if Mollie was suffering from it or anything like it.

Against that, he remembered that she had struck him as a reasonably normal woman. Not nearly as intelligent as her sister, but there had been no lack of good sense in the way that she had attempted to comfort Leslie Gleeson about the continuing mystery of her missing child. She had been calm and kindly. All the same, if she had had her bad times and Constance had had to cope with them, it was clear enough why she was so worried now.

Thrice looked he at the city;
Thrice looked he at the dead;
And thrice came on in fury...

That bloody Horatius again! After a few quiet curses, Andrew did his best to drive him out of his mind. He was not aware of going anywhere in a fury, but only into the village of Clareham, and he was not expecting to have to look at anyone dead even once, let alone three times. Reaching the crossroads, where he could see the attractive Georgian house where Dr. Pegler lived, he turned to the left and continued towards Clareham.

It was a straggle of houses along the main road to Maddingleigh. One or two small side roads branched off it, one leading down to a triangular green with a church and a school facing onto it, as well as the village hall, in which Constance had told Andrew the surgery was held twice a week. She had told him that Miss Grace lived in a small semi-detached house just beyond it. Andrew found it without difficulty and had just turned in at the gate when a blue Mini stopped in front of it. He recognized it as the nurse's car and a moment later Miss Grace came trotting briskly up the garden path after him. There was a pleasant smile on her round, blunt-featured face.

"Good afternoon," she said. "I know who you are though Mr. Ryan didn't introduce us yesterday. You're Professor Camm's friend, aren't you, and you're staying with her and Mrs. Baird? I don't know your name, but Mrs. Baird told me about you. Is there anything I can do for you?"

"My name's Basnett," Andrew answered, "and as a matter of fact I wanted to ask you something about Mrs. Baird. If you've time to spare at the moment and could give me a few minutes I'd be very grateful."

"Come in and have a cup of tea," she said. "I'm going to make one for myself. You don't know how badly I want one around this time of day. And I'm finished with my work, I'm glad to say, unless I'm called out. So come in and make yourself at home."

She unlocked her front door and led him into a small sitting room so tidy and so clean and so bright with polishing that he felt almost afraid to walk across the gleaming floor and sit down in a shiny, plastic-covered armchair.

She had taken off her blue uniform jacket and her neat little navy-blue hat, shaking loose her short grey hair that had been squashed flat by it, and in spite of Andrew's protest that she should not trouble about tea for him, as what he wanted to ask her would take only a few minutes, she disappeared into the kitchen to make the tea.

In a little while she appeared with a tea tray.

"There," she said as she handed him a cup, and subsided with a little sigh of weariness into another plastic-covered chair. "That's better." Her eyes, behind her thick round spectacles, had a gleam of curiosity in them as she surveyed him. "I need my tea. Now tell me what you want to ask me about Mrs. Baird. We're old friends, you know. In the days when I used to go up to Lindleham House to attend to poor old Mrs. Ryan after her stroke, we got to know each other very well. She was wonderful with the old woman. So patient and understanding when she got a bit difficult towards the end. Mind, I'm not saying there was anything wrong with Mrs. Ryan mentally. There wasn't. She could be as sharp as a needle when she chose. Sometimes a bit too sharp, in fact, always criticizing Mrs. Baird as if she wasn't doing her very best for her, and some of the things she used to say to me—Well!" She gave a laugh. "Of course, I'm used to old people. Half my job's with them and I don't take offence. And sometimes she used to be quite amusing. I remember once when Dr. Pegler put her on some new pills and she shouted at him, 'Pills, pills, that's all you can do for me, nothing but pills! If you picked me up and shook me, I'd rattle!' "

"I believe Mrs. Baird went into his surgery this morning to collect some pills," Andrew said.

"Did she? Yes, of course she did. I think she said that was what she'd come for. I happened to have dropped in for a few minutes to ask Dr. Pegler something and I met her there." She paused. Her eyes looked abnormally enlarged behind the thick lenses of her spectacles. "I'm sorry. You didn't come here just to hear me chatter, though I do enjoy it when I get the chance. Is something wrong with Mrs. Baird?"

"It's just that she hasn't come home since she set out to the surgery this morning," Andrew said, "and Professor Camm's troubled about her. We were told Mrs. Baird left the surgery with you and we wondered if she'd said anything to you about what she was meaning to do then."

"Yes, we left together, that's true," the nurse said, "and I gave her a lift to the crossroads. I'd a visit to make further on, a dressing to do for an old fellow with a nasty abscess, and I saw Mrs. Baird start up Bell Lane. You mean you haven't seen her since then?"

Andrew shook his head. "About what time would that have been?"

"About half past eleven, I should think, or thereabouts."

"And she didn't say anything, as far as you can remember, about calling in on anyone, or anything like that?"

"No, I just took for granted she was going straight home. Mind you..." She stopped.

"Yes?" Andrew said.

"Have some more tea," she said. "You don't know how I like my tea when I get home."

"You were going to say...?"

"Oh, nothing special." She took his cup from him and refilled it. "Professor Camm's a very clever person, isn't she?"

"Yes, indeed."

"Seems funny, somehow, a woman being a professor, but I suppose times have changed. You're old friends, aren't you?"

Andrew remembered what Constance had said about the nurse resenting her.

"Yes, we worked together in the same department for about twenty years," he said, "and she was a great friend of my wife's."

"You've lost your wife, then? You said Professor Camm was a great friend of hers."

"Yes, she died of cancer ten years ago."

"Sad, very sad. I'm so sorry. Of course, Professor Camm will be a rich woman if Mrs. Baird dies first. She inherited a lot of money from Mrs. Ryan, you know, though they like to live so modestly."

Andrew found it difficult to follow the nurse's line of thought. It seemed to him disconnected. Then the suspicion suddenly came to him that she imagined that his friendship for Constance was based on some idea of his marrying her for the money that she might acquire if Mollie were to die first. In spite of the woman's good-natured, rosy face and her cheerful smile, he began to like her less than he had at first.

"About those pills she collected this morning…" he said.

"Mild tranquilizers," she said. "She was very upset when Mrs. Ryan died. After all, she'd lived with her for fifteen years. She was almost like a daughter to her. Well, I suppose it was that that upset her. Mrs. Baird got very nervous and depressed for a time, in spite of having been left all that money. And I've sometimes wondered… Still, I mustn't gossip. I get to know a lot of things in my work, you know, but I'm very careful not to gossip."

"I'm sure you are." He did not feel sure at all. "But I mustn't keep you. I just wanted to ask you if you knew what Mrs. Baird might have done after you saw her in the surgery, but I gather you don't know any more about that than we do."

"No, and I don't wonder you're worried if you haven't seen her since then. It's certainly strange." But was there a glint of pleasure in those unnaturally enlarged eyes? "I expect it'll turn out there's some quite ordinary explanation of it. Suppose, for instance, she was asked in for lunch by some friend she met and tried to ring up Professor Camm to say she wouldn't be home for some time, but it turned out the phone was out of order and she couldn't get through. Things like that do happen and she might not have thought it would upset you much if you didn't hear from her."

"Yes, that might be possible."

"It's much more likely than that anything awful's happened. When you get back you may find she's got home already."

"I hope I do." He stood up. "Thank you for the tea and for letting me bother you with my questions."

"My pleasure. I wish I could have helped more." She stood up to open the door for him. "Actually I could tell you some things about Mrs. Baird… But it wouldn't be right, and it's got nothing to do with her not coming home today. No, I've told you all I can about seeing her today. We met in the surgery. She'd been shopping, I think. She'd a basket of groceries with her. And I gave her a lift as far as the crossroads, and we talked mostly about poor little Colin Gleeson going missing. He's been gone now about a month and my opinion is that the poor child's certainly dead. Not that I said so. The Gleesons are friends of Mrs. Baird's and I didn't want to distress her. Mr. Gleeson was in the surgery this morning and I saw her talking to him. Poor man, he must feel terrible, because everyone knows it was his fault the child ran away. I thought he was looking very poorly."

"I believe he's got a bad back, which is enough to make anyone look poorly," Andrew said. "Well, thank you, and perhaps, as you say, I may find Mrs. Baird has got home while I've been here, troubling you with my questions. You've been very patient with me."

However, when a little while later Andrew reached Cherry Tree Cottage and Constance let him in, Mollie had not returned. Constance offered to make him tea, but he assured her that he had been provided with more than enough by Nurse Grace. Constance's face had a pinched look and there were shadows of anxiety under her eyes.

"But if it isn't too early, I could do with a drink," Andrew said.

She assumed that he wanted whisky and poured it out for him, then did the same for herself. But when he went into the sitting room and sat down she remained standing in front of the empty fireplace.

"She'd nothing to tell you, of course," she said.

"I'm not sure that she hadn't," he answered. "You know, that woman knows something about Mollie. She went out of her way twice to tell me that she did and that her only reason for not saying more was that it would be unprofessional to gossip. She also said that it could have nothing to do with Mollie not coming home today, but I wondered if she was letting me know in a rather malicious way that was meant to puzzle me that she knows what Mollie did with Mrs. Ryan's will."

"It's possible," Constance said. "She and David Pegler witnessed it. If she doesn't actually know anything about how it disappeared, she may have her suspicions."

"Do you think it's possible that she's your blackmailer?"

For a moment Constance did not answer, then she said, "As it happens, I've wondered about that myself."

"But you've no evidence that points to her?"

"None at all."

"Well, now the question is: what are you going to do? Are you just going to go on waiting to see if Mollie comes back, or are you going to tell the police that she's missing?"

"Is that what you think I ought to do?"

He had not expected her to say that. He had thought that at mention of the police she might shy as she had earlier when he had advised her to show them the anonymous letter. But it was plain that now she was prepared to listen to the suggestion.

"Tell me something," he said. "You've spoken of Mollie having had a couple of breakdowns, but you didn't tell me what form they took. What actually happened to her?"

She wandered away to the window, standing there with her back to him, as if she would have liked to blot out his question. Then she gave a little shrug of her shoulders, evidently deciding that it did not matter how much he knew.

Returning to stand on the hearth rug, she said, "The first time it was simply intense anxiety and depression. She wouldn't go out of the house. The thought of it seemed to terrify her. Agoraphobia, I suppose. And she wept a great deal. But it didn't last very long. The second time was far more frightening. We were out together, having supper in a café, and I was just going to pay our bill and we were going to go home, when all of a sudden she got up and ran out. She hadn't even waited to put on her coat, she was wearing just a light blouse and skirt, and it was January and it was snowing outside, and she simply vanished into the snow. I went to the police then and they found her hiding behind a van in a car park some way off, but when they tried to persuade her to come home with me she fought and screamed and that was when I managed to arrange for her to be taken into a mental home. She was there for three months and when she came out you'd never have thought there'd been anything the matter with her. She talked about the whole experience quite rationally and told me that when she'd run away from me in the café it was because she thought she'd suddenly seen the devil looking at her out of my eyes. She was very sorry about all the trouble she'd caused and seemed to be completely back to normal. And that's what I've assumed she was until she told me about how she'd destroyed Mrs. Ryan's will. That started me worrying again, because she's always been such an honest person, it wasn't in character."

"And today you're afraid she may have seen the devil again looking at her out of your eyes, or possibly mine, and that's why she's disappeared."

She made no response for a moment, then she nodded.

"That other time it happened, I'd no warning," she said. "There we were eating our fish and chips and talking about what we might watch that evening on television, and suddenly she was gone."

"As she's gone now."

She nodded again. As she did so someone knocked on the front door.

The way that Constance's slim body jerked at the sound and that she spilled some whisky on the carpet showed how tense she was.

Andrew stood up. "I'll see who it is."

But she was out of the room ahead of him, had reached the front door before he could and had flung it open.

A tall, thin man stood on the doorstep. A little way behind him stood another man, who was shorter, thickset and younger. In the lane was a car. The tall, thin man had a long, cadaverous face which was almost rectangular, with a pointed nose, a high, narrow forehead and grave brown eyes. He gave Constance a long, questioning look before he spoke and also took a quick look at Andrew, who had an impression, for no reason that he could name, that the man was glad to see him there.

"Professor Camm?" he asked.

"Yes," Constance answered.

"I'm very sorry to have to intrude like this," the man said, "and also to have to tell you some very bad news. Perhaps if we could go inside…" He gave Andrew another glance, as if he were hoping that he would help him. "I'm Detective Superintendent Stonor and this is Sergeant Southby."

"It's about my sister Mollie," Constance said, staying where she was. Her voice was steady.

"I'm afraid so," Superintendent Stonor replied. "But may we come in? I think it might be best."

"Yes, come in," Constance said in the same calm voice. "But please tell me what's happened. Has she been in an accident?"

If Mollie had been in an accident, Andrew thought, it would not have been a detective superintendent who stood on the doorstep.

The man was still reluctant to answer while he was there, but Constance did not move aside so that he could enter.

"It wasn't an accident," he said finally. "Her body was found by two boys about an hour ago in the stream at the bottom of Clareham Hill. She'd been stabbed in the back. Stabbed several times with what we think was a kitchen knife. I'm afraid it was murder."

Chapter Five

Thrice looked he at the city;
Thrice looked he at the dead...

Andrew was thankful that he did not have to look three times at Mollie's empty, colourless face. Once was enough.

When Superintendent Stonor had told Constance regretfully that as a formality he would have to ask her to go to the mortuary in Maddingleigh with him to identify her sister, she had given Andrew a swift look and he had known that he would have to accompany her.

He took it as a matter of course that he should go, and when they were taken into the chilled room where Mollie's body, covered by a sheet, had been laid out, it had not surprised him that Constance had suddenly slipped her hand into his and had held on tight. But at the same time her calm had disturbed him. Though her hand was icy cold, her gaze at Mollie, during the moment when the sheet had been turned back, was as steady as if she were looking at a specimen in a laboratory. The brief nod that she gave when the superintendent asked her if this was her sister expressed nothing.

Andrew knew that in her way she was a very strong woman and he believed that she was capable of facing many things which would make most people crumple, but he felt that there was something desperate about this self-control and that it would have been better for her to give in to her emotions.

After they emerged from the mortuary they got back into the police car that had brought them to Maddingleigh and were driven back to Lindleham. The superintendent went with them. When they arrived at Cherry Tree Cottage he addressed Andrew.

"Do you think Professor Camm could answer a few questions now, or shall I come back later? This must have been a great shock for her."

He had been glad, as Andrew had realized when he first saw him, that Constance was not alone and particularly that it was a man who was there with her, a man with whom the detective would find it far easier to talk than with this small, old, terribly tense woman.

Andrew said, "Constance?" knowing what the answer would be.

"Now," she said. "Now. Let us deal with this at once. There are questions I want to ask you as well as what you want to ask me."

"Of course," the superintendent said. "Very well then, if we may, we'll come in with you."

His voice was quiet, with a touch of the Berkshire accent in it, and was full of sympathy. Andrew wondered how it would have sounded if Constance had refused to let him come in and to answer his questions.

She led the way into the house. The time, Andrew noticed as they passed a grandfather clock in the hall, was ten minutes past seven. That surprised him. He felt sure that it was far later. The day seemed to have been going on interminably.

Sergeant Southby followed Superintendent Stonor in and took a chair in the corner of the room, making himself as inconspicuous as possible. Constance sat down in her usual char beside the fireplace. She was very pale and the lines from her nostrils to the corners of her mouth were deeper than usual, but her eyes were as bright as ever. Almost more bright, Andrew thought, and he wondered uneasily what would happen to her once she yielded to the effect of shock. From experiences of his own he knew that it did not always make itself felt immediately. At a time of crisis many people can be totally calm, can even appear almost indifferent to what has happened, but they pay for it later.

"I think Professor Camm could do with a drink," he said to Stonor. "What about you?"

A little to his surprise, because he had been reared in the belief that policemen do not drink when they are on duty, both men accepted. Perhaps, he thought, Stonor felt that it would help Constance to relax if he joined her in a drink. It was Constance who rejected hers. She accepted the glass that Andrew filled for her, but put it down on a small table beside her and did not touch it.

"I've several things to tell you," she said. "Things that perhaps I ought to have told you before now. Professor Basnett thought I should. Perhaps if I had, this terrible thing wouldn't have happened. I don't think it would have made any difference, but who can tell? It might have. In any case, I shall always blame myself. But first will you tell me how and when you found my sister?"

She could have asked the same question when they had been in the car on their way into Maddingleigh, but she had been completely silent. Andrew wondered if she could have been trying to persuade herself that the body that she was going to see might not be Mollie's. She spoke now in as careful and precise a manner as if it had been the beginning of a lecture.

"As I told you," Stonor said, "Mrs. Baird was found—it's about two hours ago now—by two boys who'd gone fishing in the stream at the bottom of Clareham Hill. You know that hill we went down on the way into Maddingleigh. You remember we crossed a bridge over a stream there. And there's a lane branching off the main road on either side of the bridge along the side of the stream."

"I know it," Constance said.

"If you follow the lane to the left," he went on, "it eventually joins up with Bell Lane some way beyond Lindleham House, and it looks as if your sister may have been driven up Bell Lane and then along the lane towards the bridge and her body thrown into the stream about halfway along there. Then the car probably drove on to the bridge and turned towards either Clareham or Maddingleigh. You understand, so far we've only been guessing. We've had hardly any time to begin an investigation. There was no attempt to hide her identity. Her handbag was in the stream beside her and so was a basket of groceries."

"Was she alive or dead when she was driven down to the stream?" Constance asked.

"Almost certainly dead," he answered. "I'll be able to tell you more when the forensic people have had time to form an opinion, but our assumption at present is that one of the stab wounds killed her, probably around midday."

"And she'd been in the stream all that time?"

"We don't know that yet."

"But in any case, it was broad daylight when her body was thrown in. Wasn't the murderer taking a fearful risk of being seen?"

"A considerable risk, yes. We've started inquiries to see if anyone saw a car turn down into that lane or emerge from it any time from about eleven o'clock this morning onwards. But if he was aware that anyone had seen him, presumably he'd have kept the body in his car and disposed of it somewhere else. It looks as if he was in a hurry to get rid of it, otherwise he could at least have waited for darkness. There may have been a reason for that."

"I think you can narrow the time of your inquiries down at least a little," Andrew said. "This morning Mrs. Baird went to Dr. Pegler's surgery in Clareham and she left it with Nurse Grace, the district nurse, who gave her a lift to the crossroads. I had a talk with Nurse Grace this afternoon and she said it was about half past eleven when she dropped Mrs. Baird off and saw her start up Bell Lane."

"I see. Thank you," Stonor said. "That may be useful. But do I understand that you'd already started inquiries to find out what had happened to Mrs. Baird?"

"Yes," Constance said. "You see, she went along to the surgery, as she does once a month, to pick up some pills, and I expected her to come straight home. She was walking, she hadn't taken the car, but even so she'd normally have been home by twelve o'clock at the latest. But for a time when she didn't come back I thought she might be having a drink with someone, and then just possibly that she'd stayed on for lunch wherever she was, though it wasn't like her to do that without telephoning. In fact, it wasn't like her to do it at all, because she was going to do a little shopping in the village for our lunch, and we've a guest, so she was likely to be home in good time to get the lunch, as she usually did. So presently I phoned Mrs. Roberts, who's Dr. Pegler's receptionist, and asked her if she'd seen my sister, and it was she who told me she'd seen her leave with Miss Grace. So later in the afternoon, when my sister still hadn't come home, Professor Basnett went along to ask Miss Grace if she knew anything about her, and she told him about giving Mollie a lift to the crossroads. And that's the last we know about her. And as a matter of fact, we'd just been talking about getting in touch with the police when you and the sergeant arrived here."

While she had been talking Andrew had found himself wishing that her voice would shake, or that tears would appear in her eyes, but she went quietly and lucidly on. He was scared of what her reaction might be presently.

The sergeant was making jottings in a notebook. Stonor was looking at Constance with a gravity that gave his narrow, rectangular face a look of severity, but his voice remained gentle.

"Can you give us any idea why this horrible thing should have happened?" he asked.

She hesitated, then got up and went to a small bureau in a corner of the room. Opening a drawer, she took out a letter which Andrew recognized as the anonymous letter that she had shown him in his flat in London. She held it out to Stonor.

"My sister received this three days ago," she said. "Will you read it?"

He glanced at the address on the envelope, then took the letter out and read it.

"Curious," he commented.

"What do you make of it?"

"I would need some time to think about that. What did you make of it yourself?"

She sat down again. "My first guess was that it was the work of a lunatic. Then I began to think it might be just an ugly sort of hoax. Then I had another idea and when I'd thought of it I began to get scared and I went to London to see Professor Basnett, who's a very old friend, to see what he thought of it. And he agreed with me that my idea was a possible explanation of the letter. It was that someone had written two letters, probably both of them with almost the same address in Bell Lane, then had got them muddled up so that my sister got one that had been intended for someone else, while that person got a letter that had been meant for her. And I should tell you that Professor Basnett advised me to show that letter you've got there to the police immediately, but I didn't because of the other letter that someone else got. I was afraid of your finding out what was probably in it. But I don't see why I shouldn't tell you about it now. It can't hurt anyone."

"Do I understand you think it referred to your sister and that now she's dead you don't mind who knows what was in it?"

"Just that."

"Then you're going to tell me now what you think it was?"

"Yes, but you must understand, I'm only guessing. It's only a guess that there were two letters that got mixed up. I've no evidence of it. Perhaps I was right in the first place and it was just a bad joke or a bit of lunacy."

"Yes, I understand. But what is it you're afraid of?"

For the first time her hand closed round the glass on the table beside her and it looked as if she were about to drink from it. But then she let it go. Folding her hands in her lap, she said, "Do you know that my sister inherited a lot of money from Mrs. Ryan, who lived at Lindleham House, and for whom she worked for fifteen years?"

"No," he said, "I don't know anything about that."

"That was what happened," Constance said. "But there was a complication. Mrs. Ryan made the will that left the money to Mollie about a month before she died. She'd had a stroke and was semi-paralyzed. The witnesses were Dr. Pegler and Nurse Grace. There was a legacy to the housekeeper, Mrs. Grainger, and the house was left to Mrs. Ryan's nephew, Nicholas, but all the rest of her money was left to Mollie."

"Just a moment," Stonor interrupted. "Your sister saw this will? She was certain of its terms?"

"So I understood from her."

"I see. Go on."

"Well, a few days before Mrs. Ryan's death she made another will, and again the witnesses were Dr. Pegler and Nurse Grace, but neither of them knew anything about what was in it, or so they said. But Mollie told me she'd read it and that it left her and Mrs. Grainger only small legacies and everything else to Nicholas. But that will disappeared. It's never been found. It seemed possible that Mrs. Ryan destroyed it herself, doing one more last-minute change of her mind, because she did tear up some papers and got Mrs. Grainger to remove the fragments. That at least was believed at the time and so the earlier will was accepted, one reason being that Nicholas never made any attempt to contest it. And so Mollie inherited a lot of money, while Nicholas got only that ugly great house. However..." For the first time her voice shook and her hand darted out to the glass of whisky and she drank a little.

"Yes?" Stonor said.

"It was Mollie who destroyed the second will," Constance said abruptly. "She told me so herself. There, I've got that off my chest at last."

In the last few minutes the superintendent's face had become completely expressionless. There was only a blank sort of seriousness on it. He said nothing, apparently waiting for Constance to go on. He had guessed before she told him, Andrew thought, what she was going to say and he did not intend to help her now with questions.

"I told you," Constance went on, and there was a note of desperation in her voice, "she told me so herself."

"And that's all the evidence of it you have?" Stonor asked. "Her spoken word?"

"Yes, but of course it was true."

"What sort of woman was your sister?"

It took Constance a moment to decide how to reply. "She was—oh, she was—well, sometimes peculiar."

"Dishonest in many ways?"

"Oh no, not at all. Never. Very scrupulous."

"It was hardly scrupulous to destroy a will."

"No, but I've said she was peculiar. What I mean is, she'd had two serious mental breakdowns. On the one occasion she was in a mental home for some months, and when she destroyed the will I was sure—what's the phrase?—that the balance of her mind was disturbed."

"So when she told you about this, you did nothing about the matter yourself. Was the balance of your mind disturbed too?" For the first time there was an edge on his voice.

The only effect that it had on Constance was to bring the twitch of a sardonic smile to her lips.

"Do you know, I think it may have been," she said. "Certainly, on looking back, it seems to me my judgement was seriously at fault. I only thought of what I believed would be best for Mollie, and I don't mean simply in financial terms. I thought of what it might do to her if she had to confess in public what she'd done. I thought of it perhaps getting into the newspapers and of what her friends would think of her. And I thought it might easily drive her over the edge again, and then—then there was always the chance that she'd never come back. Of course, ever since the last time it's always been at the back of my mind that it could happen again. Have you ever had any contact, Mr.

Stonor, with anyone who you're deadly afraid may one day turn out to be incurably insane?"

"I meet them every day of my life," he answered. "And a good deal of my job consists of trying to decide whether they're genuine or fakes."

"I don't think you happen to love them, however," Constance said.

"No, it's true, I'm spared that." The hard edge had gone again from his voice. "So you thought it would be best for your sister if you said nothing about what she'd told you and if she said nothing either."

"Yes, but I've been certain for some time that I was wrong. It would have been far better to get the whole matter into the open and to have it cleared up. Just how one could have cleared it up legally I don't know, but I suppose it could have been done. As it was, it preyed on her mind and used to bring on attacks of depression that frightened me. And then that letter came..."

"Ah, I'm glad we're getting back to that," he said. "Do I understand you were afraid that a letter which may have been received by someone else when it was intended for your sister referred to her having destroyed that will and was an attempt to blackmail her?"

"That's what I was going to say."

"And that the letter which reached her, accusing her of murder, may mean that her murder isn't the only one we've got to consider—but I'll come back to that presently. What I'd like to ask you now is: who could have known what was in Mrs. Ryan's second will, or that your sister destroyed it? According to what you've told me, it might conceivably have been Dr. Pegler, Nurse Grace, Mrs. Grainger or Mr. Ryan. One of them could have been the blackmailer who wrote to Mrs. Baird. But is there anyone else?"

"It's possible," Constance said. "Mollie might have confided in someone besides me. And I've been thinking, if she did that, it may be a clue to why she was murdered."

"Will you explain that?"

She made a small helpless gesture with her hands.

"I can't really. It's just a feeling I have. Perhaps when she told this person about what she'd done—if she did and I don't really believe she would—she somehow made him feel that she knew more about him than he liked."

"But you've no idea what she might have said."

"None at all."

"Or when she said it."

"No."

"Do you think she met this person this morning and talked in a way that made him feel it was urgent to get rid of her?"

"That might have happened, mightn't it?"

"Do you know whom she met?"

"No, of course not. I know she talked to Dr. Pegler and Miss Grace, and I've been told Mr. Ryan and Mr. Gleeson were also in the surgery and that she chatted to them, but as she had that basket of groceries with her it meant she'd gone shopping before she went to the surgery and I don't know anything about whom she may have met while she was doing that. But to tell you the truth…"

She hesitated and he waited for her to go on.

"I can't believe she confided in anyone but me about destroying the will," she said. "It was difficult enough for her to bring herself to tell me about it. Somehow I can't really see her telling even a close friend about it."

"Which brings us back to the fact that the most likely people to have known what she'd done are the doctor, the nurse, the housekeeper and the nephew."

She nodded.

"And which of those strikes you as the most probable blackmailer?" There was a touch of irony in his voice, and Andrew began to fear that from the beginning he had not taken her seriously.

She seemed to feel it too, for there was irritation in her voice when she answered, "I can't possibly say. I'm not used to blackmail."

He stood up. "Well, thank you for your help, Professor. I'm afraid answering all my questions must have put a severe strain on you. I'm sorry. I'll keep the letter, if you don't mind. It's typewritten and that may always tell us something. Just one thing more…"

She waited.

"I don't know what, in the circumstances, is the position about Mrs. Ryan's will," he said. "We'll need a lawyer to explain that. But I presume that you inherit all that your sister had to leave."

"No," Constance said.

"You don't?"

"No, some time ago she made a will leaving everything she had to Nicholas Ryan."

He raised his eyebrows. "Did she really? You're sure of that?"

"Yes, our solicitor in Maddingleigh has the will. Peters, Clarke and Peters. But my sister had a copy of it, which I imagine is somewhere among her papers here. I'll look for it, if you like."

"Not now. We can get in touch with your solicitor tomorrow. But will you tell me, did Mr. Ryan know about the will?"

"I don't know. Perhaps Mollie told him about it."

" Do you think if she had it's something she would have told you?"

"I don't know. There've been times recently when I've felt I didn't know my sister at all. I don't know what she might have done."

"Good night, then. I hope I shan't have to trouble you tomorrow, but I'm afraid I may have to. Try to have a good rest now."

At last the two detectives left.

For a moment after they had gone Constance sat perfectly still, then reached suddenly for her glass and swallowed what was left in it at a gulp.

"I can't believe it," she said. "I can't believe any of it happened."

"Constance, if Ryan knew about Mollie's will," Andrew said, "it gives him a very powerful motive—"

But that was as far as he got. First putting down the glass with a look of great carefulness, Constance slid gently down in her chair, unconscious.

Andrew did not know what to do. During the war he had had a number of lessons in first aid, but none of them had related to what ought to be done when a woman in her seventies, who had just received a severe emotional shock, collapsed on his hands.

Was it simply a faint? If it was, he believed, the right thing to do was to bend her head downwards between her knees and keep it there until consciousness returned. But suppose it was a heart attack or a stroke? Neither at her age, and considering the strain of the last hour or so, was improbable, and if either had happened, for all he knew, moving her might be dangerous.

It did not really take him long to decide what to do, though as he stood wondering for a horrible moment if she had died while he looked at her, it felt as if he had remained there uselessly for some endless, incalculable time. But then he reached for the telephone, flipped over the pages of the pad on the table beside it till he found a note of Dr. Pegler's number and dialled it. If the doctor was not at home his answering phone would probably tell Andrew where he was to be found.

But luckily it was David Pegler himself who answered.

"This is Basnett speaking," Andrew said. "You remember, we met at the Gleesons'. Could you come to Cherry Tree Cottage at once? Constance has just collapsed. She's passed out and I don't know what to do. I don't know if you've heard the news about her sister, but the police have been here questioning Constance for a long time and it's been too much for her."

The doctor wasted no time asking questions.

"I'll be round in a few minutes," he said, and rang off.

Andrew replaced the telephone and turned back to Constance. At least she was alive, for she was breathing in a heavy, snorting way, but her face was as colourless as that of Mollie in the mortuary. She was slumped sideways in an ungainliness that seemed unnatural in someone usually so neat and collected. Andrew decided to take a risk and carry her to the sofa.

She was very light. Though he was as old as she was and past the age for attempting to lift heavy weights, he managed it easily and settled her in what looked a comfortable posture, with a cushion under her head. Then he sat down, watching her intently to make sure that the breathing went on.

He looked at his watch several times while he waited for the doctor to arrive. The minutes passed very slowly. In the silence Horatius seized the opportunity to move in on Andrew's mind.

> "For how can man die better
> Than facing fearful odds,
> For the ashes of his fathers,
> For the temples of his gods...?"

Andrew could think of all sorts of better ways of dying. His own choice would be to die in his bed with a kindly doctor in attendance who was ready to be generous in the matter of injecting morphine. But it was a curious thing to realize how seldom he had had to face anything that could be described as fearful odds. His wife's death, the months before it when they had both known that it was inevitable, and the years after it until he had adjusted himself after a fashion to his loneliness had been by far the worst thing that had ever happened to him.

His war had been a fairly peaceful one. Being a scientist and a teacher, he had been in a reserved occupation and probably his worst experience had been lecturing to a hall full of medical students to whom he had had to attempt to teach the elements of biology. He had been very young and unsure of himself and they had been bored and unruly. Later he had come to enjoy lecturing, but it had taken him some time to learn how to control a big class without any fear of it.

His most notable exploit during those years had been in an air raid, when as a member of the fire brigade of his college he had been on its roof when a firebomb had landed a few feet away from him, and using his long-handled shovel he had scooped it down into the street and had narrowly missed hitting a policeman. Since that occasion he had never had any doubt that English was the richest of languages.

> *But the Consul's brow was sad,*
> *And the Consul's speech was low,*
> *And darkly looked he at the wall,*
> *And darkly at the foe...*

The sound of the door knocker rescued Andrew from Horatius. He had been looking pretty darkly at Constance for any sign of returning consciousness, furious with himself because of his ignorance and inability to help her, and when he heard the knocker he shot out of the room as fast as he could to greet the doctor.

It was only as he did so that it occurred to him that the room was in twilight and that it was time to switch on the lights. Doing so as he went, he let David Pegler in.

"I came as quickly as I could," he said. "Where is she?"

He turned automatically to the staircase, ready to go up to her bedroom.

"No, in here," Andrew said, indicating the open sitting-room door. Although it seemed so much longer, it had in truth been only a few minutes since he had spoken to the doctor on the telephone.

Perhaps the turning on of the lights had had some effect on Constance, for her eyes were open, looking dazed and only half aware of her surroundings, but as the two men came in she started trying to sit up. Pegler put a hand on her shoulder, pressing her back against the cushions.

"Take it easy," he said. "Fainted, did you?"

He had taken her by the wrist, feeling for her pulse. The grey eyes in his round, plump face with its double chin and unusually high forehead looked at her with what Andrew thought was a surprising lack of concern. But it was possible that that was simply because he did not want to show too much, since that might have alarmed her.

"I must have," Constance said shakily. "I've never done such a thing before. I've never fainted in my life. You've heard about Mollie?"

"Mollie?" He was doing things with a stethoscope. "What's she done?"

"Then you haven't heard."

"I saw her this morning, but only for a moment. Hadn't got time to chat with her. I'd given Mrs. Roberts the usual prescription for her and I think she gave her her pills all right. Now what made you faint? Did you have any pain before it? Have you any pain now?"

"No, no, there's nothing the matter with me," Constance said impatiently. "Andrew shouldn't have called you. Andrew, please would you tell him…?"

She was beginning to look more like herself, but her voice suddenly dried up as if she could not bring herself to say any more.

Andrew told Pegler about Mollie's death, of where and when her body had been discovered, of the visit to the mortuary and the visit by the police to Cherry Tree Cottage. But he said nothing about Mrs. Ryan's will, or about Mollie having left all that she possessed to Nicholas Ryan, or about the anonymous letter that seemed to have begun everything. He hoped that that was what Constance wanted him to do. At all events, she did not add anything to what he said.

The doctor's eyes grew round with astonishment as Andrew talked. He did not interrupt, but when Andrew came to an end he muttered, "It's unbelievable. Mollie!" He clawed with a small, plump hand at his bald forehead, as if there were hair there to be thrust back. "Poor harmless Mollie! Why on God's earth can anyone have wanted to do such a thing to her?" He stared incredulously at Andrew. "Have we a maniac in our midst? Of course, as you probably know, Constance, Mollie has always been moderately unstable. She told me herself she'd spent some time in a mental home. But she seemed to have got over her trouble completely, and anyway, I don't see what that could have had to do with her murder. Could someone have imagined she was a threat to him? Could she have known something...? But no, that doesn't make sense. I'm so very sorry. I wish I could help. All I can do medically is advise you to take things as quietly as you can. I don't think there's anything the matter with you except acute stress. I'll leave you some sleeping pills—"

"No," Constance said positively. "I can manage without them. I'm sorry you've had this trouble, David. Andrew shouldn't have sent for you."

"He was quite right to do so," Pegler replied. "You've had a very bad shock, and shock can be a severe illness. It isn't everyone who's got your toughness. But for God's sake, Constance, don't be afraid of breaking down. Let it come out. You know, when Carolyn left me I began by bottling it all up inside me. I didn't want anyone to see what I was suffering. But then, when I was alone in the evening, I'd get through a bottle of whisky and the peculiar thing about it was that I stayed stone-cold sober. I wanted to get drunk, but I couldn't, and when I had to go out on calls a few times I'm certain no one noticed there was anything wrong with me. Luckily I was never stopped for a breathalyzer. But if pretty soon I hadn't taken hold of myself and said that this has got to stop, I could easily have gone on and turned into an alcoholic. And apart from killing me, given time, that would of course have been the end of my career. Not that it's much of a career, you may think. Carolyn didn't. But it's the best I can do and it means a great deal to me."

"Have you heard from Carolyn again?" Constance asked, making a visible effort to respond to Pegler instead of remaining lost in her own tragedy.

"No, I'm glad to say," he answered. "I've begun to be able to put the whole affair behind me. I think I've even begun to understand why she left me. Of course, we should never have got married. In the end this kind of thing always comes back to that. I don't blame her. She wanted more excitement than I could give her. She's just got a job that she likes, something to do with buying for a dress shop and doing some designing too, I believe, and it's going to mean travelling a good deal, which she enjoys, and she'll be making quite a lot of money. She doesn't want anything from me but a divorce. But God forgive me, why am I talking about myself like this? I suppose it may be because I've discovered how much it's helped me to let it all come out and I want you to do the same. You've a good friend here to help you." He turned back to Andrew. "Are you staying on here for any time?"

"We haven't got around to talking about that yet," Andrew said.

"Well, let me know if there's any way I can help, Constance, medical or otherwise. Don't be afraid to call me."

Pegler gave her a gentle little pat on the shoulder, picked up his bag and left.

Returning to the sitting room after closing the front door behind him, Andrew said, "I wonder if some long-tailed fish will really comfort him. You know, I can see him becoming very fond of them. But I'm sorry I called him if you'd sooner I hadn't. The fact is, you had me dead scared."

"It doesn't matter. He's a nice little man, though he's still drinking more than he says. Couldn't you smell it?" She sat up on the sofa. "Andrew, are you going to stay on here with me for a little?"

"Is that what you want me to do?" he asked.

"Please," she said.

"All right, then. Anything you want. And now hadn't you better go to bed? I'll bring you up some tea and toast, or whatever you'd like. I don't expect you feel like anything very substantial."

"I don't want anything, but you'll want something soon. I was going to cook a steak this evening, but at least there's some cold lamb in the fridge, and tomatoes and things like that. You can help yourself."

"Don't worry about it. I'm going to have another drink, then I'll look into things. What about you?"

"No, thank you."

She stood up and for a moment Andrew thought of taking her arm to see her up the stairs, but she seemed quite steady and he knew her well enough to be sure that she would not welcome support that was not needed. It was just then, however, that for the first time since Superintendent Stonor had arrived with the news of Mollie's death, Andrew saw tears in her eyes. She was not sobbing, but they were trickling quietly down her cheeks. Without making any attempt to dry them, she walked out of the room and he heard her climbing the stairs.

Pouring out a whisky for himself, Andrew sat down and gazed unthinkingly towards the uncurtained window at the end of the room. Outside, the dusk had deepened and the colours of the flowers in the garden had faded into an indistinct pattern of greys. The branches of the old walnut tree were dark against a sky which was still faintly opalescent, with an occasional star gleaming here and there. Something that the doctor had said had stirred a question in Andrew's mind, but now he could not remember what it had been. His memory was becoming shockingly bad, and at his age he could only expect it to get worse and worse.

It roused a feeling of rebellion in him that old age should deprive him of a faculty which he had always taken for granted was his for life. He had always had a very good memory. That was why he had been plagued throughout the years with the bad verse that he had enjoyed in his childhood. None of that, unfortunately, was showing any sign of fading.

The darkness outside grew deeper. He could no longer see the walnut tree or the stars because the glass of the window reflected the lights and the interior of the room. All the blank-faced Staffordshire dogs that Mollie had collected stared empty-eyed across it. But it suddenly occurred to him that although it was some time since Constance had left the room, he could still hear her moving about upstairs. She had not gone to bed. The room over the sitting room, he believed, was Mollie's, and Constance seemed to be walking about in it.

He hesitated, thinking that probably he ought to go upstairs to persuade her to leave that room and not shut herself up there alone with heaven knew what pain and perhaps what feelings of guilt. But even as he considered going up to her, he heard her coming down the stairs.

When she came into the room he saw that her tears had stopped. She was wearing a dark-blue silk dressing gown and velvet slippers and looked very small and old and fragile.

"I've been going through Mollie's desk, looking for these," she said. She held one out to him. "That's a copy of her will. The original, as I told that man Stonor, is with our solicitor in Maddingleigh, but this is the copy he sent us. However, this is what I was really looking for." She held out another paper. "It's the last letter Mollie had from Kenneth Eckersall. It came over a year ago, but it's got his address and telephone number and I don't think he's moved since he wrote. I'm going to telephone him."

"Why?" Andrew asked.

"Have you forgotten the letter she got, accusing her of murder?"

"Of course not."

"And we think it could mean that someone has been murdered."

"Possibly."

"But we don't know who."

"No."

"Then don't you understand? I want to start some elimination. I want to check up which of the people who've disappeared from Lindleham are still alive, because if we can find out who the victim is, it may give us a clue to the murderer. Because I think the only possible reason for Mollie's murder is that somehow she let the murderer know about that letter and he thought that it told her far more than it did."

"And your reason for wanting to telephone Kenneth Eckersall is simply to find out if his old father is really with him and not buried six foot deep in the Eckersalls' garden."

"Yes, and of course to tell him that Mollie's dead," she said. "He was very fond of her, you know. And actually I was wondering if you'd do the telephoning for me. I feel—well, as if I might go to pieces while I'm trying to talk. Here's his number, as I said, and the code number for Adelaide is in the book."

Andrew felt an intense dislike of undertaking what she wanted him to do, but did not see how he could refuse her. He looked up the code number in the telephone directory, read the number on the letter from Kenneth Eckersall and dialled. The connection was made almost immediately. He heard the clear ringing tone of the telephone in that house at the other end of the earth, but nobody answered.

"Constance!" he exclaimed suddenly. "We can't go on with this. Have you any idea what the time is over there? It's probably the middle of the night and they're sound asleep."

"It won't hurt them to be woken up for once for something as important as this," she said calmly. "Hold on and see what happens."

The ringing tone went on without bringing any response. Then all of a sudden a voice exploded in Andrew's ear.

"What the bloody hell d'you think you're doing, ringing up at this hour of the morning?"

"Is that Mr. Eckersall?" Andrew asked.

"It is, and who the hell are you?" The voice was faintly tinged with an Australian accent, which Kenneth Eckersall must have acquired during the past years.

"My name won't mean anything to you," Andrew answered, "but I'm a friend of Mrs. Baird's and Professor Camm's and I'm staying in Lindleham—"

"Hey, is there anything the matter with my sisters? Is that why you're phoning?" The voice sounded anxious, less aggressive.

"To the best of my belief there's nothing the matter with either of them," Andrew replied, "but I have some very grave news about Mrs. Baird, who I believe was a friend of yours. Constance Camm wanted me to telephone—"

"*Was* a friend of mine," the voice took him up quickly. "D'you mean something's happened to Mollie?"

"Yes, a very terrible thing," Andrew said. "Her body was found today in a stream near Clareham. Constance wanted me to tell you she's dead."

"*Dead?*"

"Yes."

"Mollie? You really mean Mollie's dead?"

"Yes." But this was not bringing Andrew any nearer to finding out whether or not the old father of the Eckersalls was safe and sound in the home of his son. "Would it be possible for me to speak for a moment to your father? I believe he and Mollie were very attached to one another."

It was the best excuse that he could think of on the spur of the moment for wanting to speak to the old man.

"Not specially," the son said, "and you can't speak to him because he isn't here. Mollie dead! What was it—an accident? She was a rotten driver."

"No."

"Not suicide!"

"To tell you the worst straightaway, Mr. Eckersall," Andrew said, "she was stabbed to death and her body was thrown into a stream. You say your father isn't with you?"

"No, I should think he's in Fiji by now. He's on his way home via Fiji, Los Angeles and New York, taking it slowly, seeing a bit of the world while he still can. He left yesterday, though I'm damned if I see why you want to talk to him. He'll be home in a couple of weeks. You're telling me Mollie was murdered."

"Yes."

"Who did it?"

"Nothing is known about that yet."

"Why could anyone have wanted to do such a thing?"

"People don't always seem to need reasons, do they?"

There was a momentary pause, then Kenneth Eckersall asked quietly, "Look, are you really a friend of Mollie's and Constance's, or are you a policeman, checking up on me and my father for God knows what reason?"

"No, I'm not a policeman," Andrew said. "My name's Basnett—Andrew Basnett—and Constance and I worked together for twenty years. I happened to be staying with her and Mollie when this appalling thing happened. As I told you, Constance wanted me to tell you about it. I'm afraid we just forgot about the time difference."

"That's all right. I'm glad you called. Thanks." Kenneth Eckersall sounded very subdued now. "Give my sympathy to Constance, will you, and if they find out anything..."

"Yes?"

"I'd be glad if you let me know about it."

"I'll do that."

Andrew put the telephone down. He turned to Constance, who was sitting on the edge of a chair, watching him and listening intently.

"I'm afraid you can't eliminate old Mr. Eckersall as your possible victim," he said. "His son claims he's in Fiji at the moment, on his way home. That may or may not be true. If he and his sisters were in this thing together there's a possibility that the old man never went to Australia at all."

She sighed. "No, and I can't see how we can eliminate any of the others who've disappeared, unless possibly Carolyn. I wonder if I could get her phone number from David, or perhaps from some friend of hers. She was quite close friends with the Wakehams. Naomi might know where she is."

"But even that would leave you with Naomi's husband, who may or may not be in MI5, or a drug smuggler, and a little boy who's been missing long enough for it to be rather likely that he's dead. You know, the number of young children who disappear is quite unspeakable. They're such easy victims—"

He stopped as he heard the sound of someone walking quickly up the garden path, then pounding with the knocker on the front door.

Chapter Six

Constance stood up quickly.

"Please," she said, "see to it for me. I couldn't take anyone now."

"All right," Andrew said. "You go upstairs. I'll see to it."

She went out swiftly and he heard her hurrying up the stairs. When he was sure that she had reached the top he went to the front door and opened it.

Naomi Wakeham stood there. She was in the green-and-white-striped shirt and the green jeans in which he had seen her before and in the light that fell on her from the hall her fair hair had a golden gleam. Her large dark eyes were wide with apprehension.

"This is awful," she said. "Awful. The police have been to see me. They told me what happened to Mollie and they asked me all kinds of questions. I came to see how Constance is. I thought you might have left and that she'd be all alone."

"That was kind of you." He stood aside so that she could come in. "She's gone to lie down. If you don't mind, I think it'll be best if we don't disturb her."

"Of course." She walked into the sitting room. "I won't stay a moment. I only wanted to say, if there's anything I can do..." However, she dropped into a chair as if she did not mean to leave immediately. "You know, I could do with a drink, if that isn't too much trouble."

"Whisky?" he asked.

"Oh, anything you've got. Gin, vodka, anything. But whisky would be fine."

He gave her a whisky and water and poured out one for himself. He realized that this evening he was drinking more than he was accustomed to, but perhaps the circumstances were a good reason for it.

It slightly shocked him to become aware just then of the fact that he was hungry. At a time such as this surely it would be proper to be indifferent to food. But he thought of the cold lamb that Constance had told him was in the refrigerator and wished that he could help himself to some of it instead of to this additional drink that he did not really want.

"What sort of questions did the police ask you?" he said as he sat down on the sofa.

"Oh, when I'd last seen Mollie and where I was this morning and all that sort of thing." She gulped hastily at her drink. She was leaning back in her chair with her long legs in their tight-fitting jeans stretched out before her, crossed at the ankles. "I think they're going all round Lindleham, asking everyone if they saw anything suspicious and asking us all for our alibis. Alibis! Honestly, isn't that fantastic? They actually asked where I was about the time they think Mollie was killed, as if I could possibly have done it. I mean, how could I have got her into my car, stabbed her several times and then bundled her out into the stream? I understand that's what happened to her, more or less. I'm quite a healthy specimen, but I couldn't have managed a thing like that. Anyway, not single-handed, and they didn't ask if there'd been anyone with me this morning. I suppose, if there had been, they'd have assumed I'd have lied about it, as I suppose I should. That would only have been natural."

"And was there anyone with you this morning?" Andrew asked.

"Of course not. Well, I mean to say, would I have said anything like that to you, putting ideas into your head, if there had been? No, I did see Mollie in the village shop and I told them that, and then I saw her at the crossroads, and I told them about the car I saw in the lane, but that's all. Alibis! If that's how they go about things it's too ridiculous. D'you think they're asking the poor old Eckersalls for their alibis?"

"It wouldn't surprise me," Andrew said. "It's mostly just a formality, but they've got to do it. But you say you did see Mollie this morning."

"Yes, I went into Smither's, the shop in Clareham, this morning, and she was there, buying odds and ends. And we chatted for a few minutes. She said she was going on to the surgery and I said I was going to have coffee with Colonel and Mrs. Bridges—they're some people who live in Clareham—and we talked about the Gleeson child. She told me how Leslie and Jim had to go and identify a little boy yesterday who'd been murdered and found in the river beyond Maddingleigh, but it wasn't Colin, and how Leslie was going nearly out of her mind. And I agreed it was one of the most horrible things I'd ever heard of, though of course I've got my own troubles too. But I didn't think it was the time to talk about those."

"You've still no news of your husband?" Andrew asked.

"Not a word. I'm becoming more and more convinced he's been sent to somewhere like one of those awful South American countries where they murder everybody, or perhaps to China or somewhere like that, and that probably I shall never hear of him again, though perhaps MI5 or 6, or whoever they are, will very secretly send me a posthumous medal or something. D'you think they'd do that? After all, I'd be a sort of war widow, wouldn't I? I wonder if I'd get a pension." Her face brightened momentarily at the thought.

"And how did Mollie strike you when you talked to her?" Andrew asked. "Quite normal?"

"Oh, absolutely. That's one of the things that makes it so shattering. I mean, I never dreamt for a moment of any doom hanging over her. But I'm not clever at that sort of thing. I mean, there are people who'd have known just by intuition that she was in some kind of awful danger. But I'm not like that. The day Mike disappeared I just kissed him goodbye as usual at the station when he left to go off to the City, then I went home and did some washing, I think, and I never dreamt I'd never see him again. And on the whole I'm glad I can't foresee things. I think it must be terribly frightening to see into the future, don't you?"

"If one really could, yes, terrifying. But you saw Mollie again later that morning?"

"Oh, just for a moment. At the crossroads. I was driving home after I'd left the Bridges—I didn't stay with them long—and I saw her get out of Lorna Grace's car and stand there looking as if she wasn't sure where she was going next. So I called out to her would she like a lift home, though of course it's only a few hundred yards, but she shook her head and I left her standing there. And that's the last I saw of her."

There was something about this narration that did not fit with the picture in Andrew's mind of what had happened to Mollie that morning, but what it was eluded him. It confirmed what the nurse had told him about her having given Mollie a lift to the crossroads and left her there, but there was something wrong with it.

"You said you saw a car in the lane," he said. "Was that on your way out or your way home?"

"Oh, coming home. It was parked almost opposite the Eckersalls' gate. A grey Vauxhall, fairly old, with a man in it. But I didn't pay much attention to it because I thought it was probably someone who'd taken a wrong turning at the crossroads and was wondering where he could turn to get back there. I don't know how long it had been in the lane, or how long it stayed after I had passed it."

"Could you describe the man to the police?"

"Oh, heavens, no. I just had a glimpse of him as I passed, and as I said, I didn't pay him any attention."

"But it was definitely a man?"

"Yes, I feel pretty sure of that."

"And it wasn't anyone you know?"

"Oh no."

"And you'd never seen the car hereabouts before?"

She swilled the whisky around in her glass, looking into it thoughtfully before taking another swallow.

"Well, the queer thing is, I feel I may have seen it some time or other," she said. "But not recently. I don't know why I feel that. It isn't as if I'm particularly observant about things like cars. It was just by chance that I recognized it was a Vauxhall, because we used to have one ourselves before we got our present car and I think this was the same model as our old one. But I could be wrong about that. Tell me, have they any idea why poor Mollie was killed?"

"They didn't tell you anything?"

"No."

"My impression is they don't know anything yet."

"And you and Constance, you haven't any ideas?"

He did not answer, and after a moment she exclaimed, "Oh dear, I'm being inquisitive! I ought not to have asked you a thing like that. I'm sorry. But I can't help wondering about it, you know. I expect you can understand that. I suppose you don't think…" She paused, finishing her whisky, then peering frowningly into the empty glass.

"Yes?" Andrew prompted her.

"Oh, it's nothing," she said. "It's just that I'm a woman alone and I've never been frightened of that before, but now that this has happened to Mollie, which must—it simply *must*—have been the work of a maniac, and thinking of that man in the car, sitting there so still and not going anywhere—oh, I'm just being stupid. Don't take any notice of me. I'll leave you in peace now. But please tell Constance how very, very sorry I am this thing has happened and that I do so wish I could help."

She stood up. Andrew stood up too.

"Mrs. Wakeham, if you're really scared of staying in that house by yourself, which is understandable," he said, "why not move into a hotel for a few days? Is there a pub in Clareham that lets rooms? If not, perhaps you could go into Maddingleigh."

She gave an unexpected little giggle. "It sounds so funny, your calling me Mrs. Wakeham. But your generation do that, don't they? They're so formal. You should call me Naomi. No, I told you I was just being stupid. I'm not as scared as all that."

"Anyway, I'll see you home," he said.

"No, don't do that. Good night. Take care of Constance."

She hurried out of the room and let herself out at the front door. He heard her footsteps on the garden path again as she made for her home.

He could get himself something to eat now. He was feeling hungrier than ever. Perhaps, he thought, it was a nervous hunger, his way of reacting to the events of the day and so not as improper as he felt that it was. But it felt normal enough. He could easily have eaten the steak which Constance had told him had been intended for dinner that evening. However, cold lamb would be better than nothing.

He went out to the kitchen, but once he was there he decided that even though Constance had said that she wanted nothing, he would make her some tea. It might do her some good and could not do any harm. He filled the kettle, found some tea things and put them on a tray and when the tea was made carried it upstairs.

He knocked on the door and Constance called, "Come in."

She had not gone to bed but was sitting in a chair by the window with only a small lamp on a table beside her lighting up the room. She was still in her dressing gown and had her hands folded in her lap.

She smiled at him. "You're very kind, Andrew, but you shouldn't have bothered."

"Drink it," he said. "It may do some good."

"Perhaps it will. Thank you."

He put the tray down on the table at her side and said, "Good night."

"Good night," she answered. Then as he was just about to leave the room, she asked, "Did Naomi come for anything special?"

"I don't think so. Offered sympathy, of course. And told me about a mysterious man in a grey Vauxhall she'd seen in the lane this morning. I'll tell you all about it tomorrow."

She nodded and as he went out was reaching for the teapot to pour out the tea.

He returned to the kitchen, cut a few slices off the joint of cold lamb that he found in the refrigerator, took two tomatoes out of a bag that he found in it, cut a thick slice of bread and buttered it, found a knife and fork and went back to the sitting room.

The windows at each end of the room were slabs of darkness. He drew the curtains to hide them, feeling as he did so that he was shutting out some menace that lurked in the pretty garden among the delicate flowers of May, and settled down on the sofa to eat his supper.

As he did so he thought of the small, old, lonely figure that he had left in the room upstairs and suddenly wondered how he would have been feeling in the situation in which he found himself if he and Constance had been twenty, even ten years younger. What would they have expected of one another? What uncertainties would they have felt? What would they have felt might be demanded of them? What extra comfort might they have been able to give one another? As it was, their age gave a kind of simplicity, a sort of uncomplicated serenity to their relationship.

The cold lamb was tender and the hunk of bread was fresh. He wondered if he could have found any pickles in the kitchen if he had looked for them. A few pickled onions would have been pleasant. But it did not seem worth his while now to look for them. He finished his meal, put the empty plate down on a table near him and leant back in his chair, suddenly feeling extremely tired. That was one of the troubles about being as old as he was. You got tired so easily. Not that a day such as the one that he had just experienced might not have drained the vitality out of most people. He would go to bed soon. Meanwhile, he let his eyelids fall, feeling a sense of peaceful relaxation.

The next moment he was sitting upright in his chair, startled by the thought that had just come into his mind. He had known that there was something that Naomi Wakeham had said to him about seeing Mollie that morning that had somehow felt wrong. He had doubted something that she had said, had felt that it contradicted something that someone else had said, yet he could not have told at the time what it was. Now he understood it.

But it was only a very little thing and perhaps did not mean anything. All the same, at the moment it might be important to take note of anything that conflicted with anything else that he had been told as to Mollie's actions. And what Naomi had said certainly conflicted, if only in a small way, with what had been said to him by Lorna Grace.

The nurse had said that she had given Mollie a lift to the crossroads, had put her down there and had seen her start up Bell Lane. But Naomi had said that she had seen Mollie get out of the nurse's car and remain standing at the crossroads, as if she could not make up her mind where she wanted to go, that in passing her Naomi had called out to her, offering a lift for the short way back to her home, that Mollie had shaken her head and that Naomi had then driven on, leaving Mollie where she was.

Indeed, a very small conflict of evidence. But one or other of the two women was wrong, either by accident or deliberately. It seemed almost certain that it was by accident, and if so it was Naomi's statement, which was slightly the more detailed, which Andrew thought was the more likely to be accurate. The nurse could easily have left Mollie at the roadside and simply have taken for granted, as she drove on, that Mollie was about to start up Bell Lane. She might not have looked back, in fact was unlikely to have done so, to make sure that Mollie had really gone. But suppose either Nurse Grace or Naomi Wakeham was lying deliberately, what could that mean?

Andrew could not think of any answer to that, and relaxing once more, he let his eyes close and drifted into a half-doze, out of which he was startled by another knock at the front door.

This time it was Jean and Kate Eckersall. As they had been when he had seen them before, they were wearing their voluminous brown smocks and one had emerald-green ankle socks on and the other cherry-red. Their dog was on the doorstep between them. Andrew could not remember which of the sisters was which, but he thought it was Jean who wore the green socks and who said now in a cautious whisper, quite unlike her normal hearty bellow, "I know it's late, terribly late, but we couldn't go to bed before coming over to see how dear Constance was, and we saw there was a light in the window downstairs, so we knew someone was up still, and we thought we'd just look in to say that if there's anything we can do, she should rely on us."

Andrew imagined that there had probably never been a time when so many people had been anxious to do things for Constance, but the chances were that she would turn to none of them. The dog, showing great pleasure at meeting Andrew again, looked as if he too would gladly offer help.

"It's very kind of you," he said. Then because it seemed the polite thing to do, he added, "Won't you come in?"

"Oh dear, we really shouldn't," Jean went on in her soft, whispering voice. It was as if she felt that if she allowed herself to speak in her normal voice it might alarm somebody. "We don't want to be a nuisance. But the police have been to see us, asking questions, and we thought perhaps we should tell Constance about it—that is, if she can bear to see anyone just now. If she'd sooner not, of course we shall understand."

"She's gone up to bed," Andrew said, "but perhaps you can tell me about the police, then I can tell her in the morning."

"Well, if you really think so…"

Walking almost on tiptoe, they crept into the sitting room. The dog followed them in and started to investigate the room.

"Oh dear, I do hope you don't mind him," Jean said.

"Not in the least."

Andrew did not feel that they were expecting to be offered a drink, so he did not do so.

They sat down in chairs on either side of the fireplace.

"You see, we've got a theory," Jean said. As Andrew had noticed before, she was very much the more articulate of the two. "We didn't tell the police about it because we only thought of it after they'd gone. At the time we'd really nothing to tell them. We hadn't seen Mollie since we got back from the Highlands. And they just told us the dreadful news and asked if we'd seen her in the lane this morning, or anyone else, and things like that. And they asked where we'd been all the morning ourselves. That seemed extraordinary, but of course we do understand they've got their duty to do and we realize that Kate and I together would have been capable of overpowering Mollie and bundling her body into our car and putting her in the stream, so it was natural they should want to check on us. And they don't know us, so they can't take for granted we'd no possible motive for doing such a thing. But after all, as we pointed out to them, if we did murder her we'd never have done anything so risky as taking her down to the stream and leaving her there. We've plenty of room to bury her in our garden and we're both quite accustomed to digging. We thought that argument made an impression on them, even though we've no alibis."

"I'm sure it did," Andrew said. "And you were at home all the morning, were you?"

"Yes, and we were together in the garden, which is an alibi of sorts, I suppose, but they wouldn't rely on it, would they, any more than they rely on the ones that are given by husbands and wives, because of course we'd lie to protect each other."

"I wonder, were you in your front garden or out at the back?" he asked.

Kate made one of her rare remarks. "As a matter of fact, a bit of both. But why?"

"Well, if you were near your gate," he said, "I was curious if you happened to see a grey Vauxhall parked near it. Some time around half past eleven, I should think. I've been told about it and it's just possible that it might have something to do with Mollie's murder."

Both sisters shook their heads.

"I didn't see anything," Jean said.

"Neither did I," said Kate.

"Do you think you'd have seen it if it had been there?"

They looked at each other uncertainly, then Jean said, "I think so. Of course, one can't be sure of a thing like that. We were coming and going. Who was in it?"

"A man. That's all I know."

They shook their heads again.

"We didn't see him," Jean said. "But if he was there only for a short time it might easily have been when we were out at the back. But d'you know, the police asked us the same question and they asked us too if we'd a typewriter and when we said we had they wanted each of us to type a specimen on it, but they didn't tell us why. What's this man in the car supposed to have had to do with Mollie's murder?"

"Perhaps nothing at all," Andrew said. "I think it's just that he might have seen her come up the lane, perhaps alone or perhaps with someone else. That might tell us something."

"Yes, I understand. As a matter of fact…" It was Kate who spoke now and she stopped, looking again at her sister as if for permission to go on.

Jean nodded and said, "Yes, there's that."

"As a matter of fact," Kate repeated, "a man who used to live next door before the Gleesons bought the cottage and put in central heating and everything, a man called Banks, who went to prison for receiving stolen scrap iron, used to have a grey

Vauxhall. But I can't think what he'd have been doing here. He left Lindleham at least three years ago and we haven't seen him since. There must be lots of grey Vauxhalls about. This man had probably just lost his way."

"Yes," Andrew agreed. "But you said you'd a theory about Mollie's death."

"I'm afraid it's rather complicated," Jean said apologetically.

"I'd be very interested to hear about it, however," he said.

"Well, there's only one possible reason we can think of why anyone should want to murder Mollie," Jean went on, "and that's that quite accidentally she found out something about somebody which was very dangerous for him. I say accidentally, because I'm sure if she understood what she knew she'd have gone to the police with it. But we think we know what it was."

Looking at her blankly, Andrew wondered if Mollie could have told the sisters about the anonymous letter, which Constance thought Mollie might have mentioned to the man who murdered her. He did not think it was likely. Besides, Jean had said that they had not seen Mollie since they had returned from the Highlands. Of course, that might not be true.

"Can you tell me about it?" he asked.

"It's about that child Colin," Jean said. "We've always had a kind of feeling that Jim Gleeson might have murdered him. We've never said anything about it before because, as I said, it was just a feeling. We never had any real evidence. But you see, it seems so probable. After all, the child is certainly dead, and infuriating as he was to a lot of people, I think the only person who really hated him was Jim, and the story that he ran away could so easily have been made up to calm poor Leslie's suspicions. And we think Mollie must have known something about it without realizing it, but today she said something that frightened him. She did see him this morning, didn't she?"

"I believe they met in Dr. Pegler's surgery," Andrew said, wondering how the sisters knew this.

Jean explained it. "We thought they must have met because the police asked us if we'd seen Jim Gleeson in the lane, or

Nicholas Ryan, or anybody else. But of course, it couldn't have been Nicholas."

"Why not?" Andrew asked.

"For the same reason it couldn't have been us," Jean replied. "He's got a great big garden. I said if we wanted to dispose of a body we'd do it in our garden, didn't I, and not risk being seen taking it along the lane to the stream. The same applies to Nicholas. His garden's much bigger than ours and there'd have been no one in the house but Mrs. Grainger to see what he was doing, and anyway there are lots of places in the garden you can't even see from the house. We know that quite well because we used to visit Mrs. Ryan quite often while she was still able to see visitors. But the Gleesons have a fairly small garden, so it would have been quite a risk for Jim to bury Mollie there. Besides, Leslie would have been sure to see what he was doing and I don't think she would go along with murder."

"I believe she was in Maddingleigh at some sale in the town," Andrew said. The Eckersalls' theory intrigued him, even though he felt that there was something the matter with it. "Suppose you're right that Gleeson killed the boy, how do you suppose he disposed of the body?"

The sisters exchanged another of their almost conspiratorial glances, then Jean said, "That's really the most interesting part of our theory."

"You think you know?"

"Have you been to the Gleesons' house?"

"Yes, for drinks yesterday evening."

"And did you notice a rose bed outside their sitting room window?"

"No, I can't say I did."

"Well, there is one there, but the roses were only planted in it about a month ago. Just about the time Colin disappeared. But quite the wrong time of year for planting roses, so of course they've come to nothing. Leslie asked me about it at the time. She said she was sure it was wrong, but that Jim insisted on doing it. And of course he'd had to dig the bed over beforehand,

and some more digging wouldn't have looked suspicious. And what we think is that if you dug down deep enough between those roses you might find Colin's body buried there."

"How was it that Leslie didn't see him do it?" Andrew asked.

"She goes out quite often in the evenings," Jean replied. "The Women's Institute and I think she goes to pottery classes and that sort of thing. He'd have had plenty of time to do it."

Andrew had a curious experience at that moment. The faces of the two sisters seemed suddenly to dissolve into something that he found startlingly frightening. For an instant the two square, tanned, good-natured faces might have been those of witches, brooding over a spell, searching his expression to see how it was working. But almost at once the absurd impression faded.

"You see, we think Mollie may have spoken to him about his roses," Jean said. "She could have said something quite innocent, like what had he been using for fertilizer, and he could have thought it was a hint that she knew what he'd got buried there. So he decided he'd got to kill her. But he couldn't put her body into the rose bed too or suddenly start digging in some other part of the garden without it seeming peculiar. But if, as you say, Leslie was in Maddingleigh this morning, he could have persuaded Mollie to go into the house with him for a drink or something, killed her there, put her body in the boot of his car and driven off with it and got rid of it in the stream. Don't you see? It all fits together."

Andrew thought that it fitted together remarkably well. But just then the brown dog, which had been lying peacefully at his feet as if he felt particularly at home there, got up, stretched and laid his head on Andrew's knee, expecting to be petted. Automatically Andrew gave him a scratch behind his ears and the dog gave a responsive wag of his tail.

It brought a memory sharply back to Andrew, the memory of four little graves in a row under a chestnut tree, all with headstones except one, and all except one with well-mown turf over them. But on one the turf had only just been laid on what must have been freshly dug earth. Jim Gleeson was not the only person who had been doing some digging recently.

When the Eckersalls had gone Andrew took his plate out to the kitchen, then went to bed. He slept restlessly. Usually he slept very well, but that night it was only in snatches and they were hagridden by dreams. The dreams in themselves did not seem to be significant or disturbing, but they made his sleep seem shallow. In one of his waking moments he wondered if Mollie had been unaware of what was to happen to her, or if for an instant she had seen the devil looking at her out of eyes that she knew.

Some time in the night he realized that a wind had arisen that battered his windows and drove an occasional spattering of rain against them. So the fine weather of the last week had come to an end. When he got up in the morning it was not raining, but the sky was grey, the wind was still blowing, and he saw that much of the blossom of the cherry tree by the gate had been torn off and lay in drifts on the grass below it. The time was eight o'clock. There was no sound of Constance moving about in the house, so he decided to go down and get breakfast for them both. He shaved, showered and dressed in trousers, a shirt and a pullover and went downstairs.

He made coffee and toast and while he was doing it helped himself to a small portion of some cheese that he found in the refrigerator. For him that was the proper way to begin a day. He had now had his small helping of protein, which he was sure would do him good. He had no need to take Constance's break-fast up to her, however, for as he was arranging it on a tray she appeared in the kitchen doorway.

She was in the dark-blue silk dressing gown in which he had seen her the evening before. Her face was colourless and seemed more deeply lined than he had ever noticed, and there was less than the usual brightness in her eyes. He wondered if she had had any sleep at all, or indeed if she had been to bed. Perhaps she had sat up all night in the chair by the window, listening to the rising wind and watching the raindrops slithering down the glass.

"I'd have got breakfast," she said. "You shouldn't have bothered."

"That's all right," he answered. "Where would you like it? In here, or shall I take it into the dining room?"

"Let's have it in here."

She advanced into the kitchen and sat down at the table. Andrew dismantled the tray that he had prepared, poured out coffee for them both, moved toast and marmalade towards her and sat down also. She picked up her cup, holding it in both hands as if she wanted to feel the warmth of it, and sipped a little.

"What did those people want last night?" she asked. "Naomi and the Eckersalls."

"Officially they all came to offer sympathy," he said, "but I've a feeling they wanted information too. And whether that was just normal curiosity or something more I wouldn't like to say."

"D'you know, Andrew, you've a very suspicious mind," she said. "I've never noticed it about you before. What more might it be?"

"Oh, I haven't thought that out. I just feel this is a good time to be suspicious on principle. And they all had information to impart. Perhaps that was what really brought them."

He told her about the grey Vauxhall with the man in it that Naomi claimed to have seen near the Eckersalls' gate, and the Eckersalls' theory about the murder of the child Colin, and Mollie's possible remarks to Jim Gleeson about roses that had been planted at the wrong time of year.

Constance did not seem much impressed. She dismissed with a slight shake of the head the suggestion that Colin might be buried in the rose bed behind the Gleesons' house, considered the presence of the Vauxhall in the lane, then shook her head again.

"It couldn't have had anything to do with Mollie," she said, "unless the man was someone she knew. If it was and somehow he persuaded her to get into the car and for some reason she let him drive her away to some place where he could murder her, I suppose he might have had something to do with it. But I can't think of any reason why he should do that unless he's a maniac, and I can't think of anyone we know who's got a grey Vauxhall."

"The Eckersalls said there was a man called Banks who used to live in the Gleesons' cottage who had one," Andrew said.

"I don't know anything about that. He left before my time. But from what I've heard of him, I don't think Mollie would have got into his car or agreed to go anywhere with him. Though, heaven knows, if he'd had some tale of woe and played on her sympathy, she might have gone. She was incurably kind. But he'd still have to be mad."

"One idea about this man seems to be that he may have seen someone with Mollie when she came along the lane and could tell the police something useful."

"I suppose that's possible. And I think to some extent the Eckersalls may be right. Someone who was scared by some knowledge he thought she had persuaded her to go into his house with him for a quick drink, then when he'd killed her there he realized that he'd got to get rid of her body in a hurry, so he put her into his car and took the risk of driving down to the stream with it. And that points pretty conclusively to Jim Gleeson. He'd have wanted to get rid of Mollie before Leslie got back from Maddingleigh. I suppose she'd gone in by bus and he knew what bus she'd come back on. The only thing is, Mollie didn't know anything about Colin and I don't feel at all convinced Jim murdered him, and even if he did, I can't really think any casual chat about roses would have made Jim think Mollie knew it."

"Of course, it's uncertain she came up the lane at all," Andrew said. "Naomi says she saw her standing at the crossroads, looking uncertain where to go. The nurse says she saw her start up the lane, but she may just have taken for granted Mollie was going to do that and driven on without actually seeing her go."

"And where do you suppose Mollie went in that case? To Pegler's?"

"Is it impossible?"

Constance reached for the coffeepot and poured out more coffee for herself. "Impossible? No. And his surgery ends at eleven, and if she knew he was going home after that and she wanted to talk to him without letting me know about it, she might have thought of going to his house and waiting for him."

"Why should she do that?"

"She may have wanted to talk to him about me."

"About you? Is there something the matter with you, Constance?"

"Not really. About a couple of months ago I had a mild heart attack and Mollie's been terribly worried about it, far more worried than I am. She wanted me to go to a consultant in London, when I was quite satisfied with the people in Maddingleigh. And if the surgery was more than usually busy this morning, she may have thought she'd try to see David after it because she wanted to discuss the matter with him. According to him, he didn't see her. But if, while she was waiting, she saw something that told her something about Carolyn—oh no, I can't believe it! I'm sure David hasn't harmed Mollie. I'd sooner believe it was Jim, or even Nicholas."

"The Eckersalls say it couldn't have been Nicholas because, like them, he's got such a big garden which isn't overlooked by anyone that he could easily have hidden Mollie's body there instead of risking taking it down to the stream."

"But if he was being very subtle, and he is a subtle character, you know, he could have counted on our thinking like that and decided to take the risk."

"The same could apply to the Eckersalls."

"So it could. Which makes my argument seem rather absurd. Oh—!" She broke off as the front door knocker sounded. "Could you see who that is, Andrew? It may be the police again. I'll run upstairs and get dressed. I shan't be a minute."

She hurried out of the kitchen.

It was not the police, it was Nicholas Ryan. As Andrew opened the door to him he became aware that he had no slippers on and was in his socks. It was a sign, he supposed, of how at home he felt with Constance that he had not noticed it till then, but as he took Nicholas into the sitting room he suddenly felt as if he were half unclothed and in some obscure way at a disadvantage.

Nicholas was in his grey trousers and black sweater, with a scarlet windcheater over them. His dark hair was windblown and the wind had whipped colour into the hollow cheeks under his slanting cheekbones.

"It's early, I know, but can I see Constance?" he asked. "There's something I've decided I've got to talk to her about."

"She'll be down in a few minutes," Andrew replied. "Sit down. Would you like some coffee? We've just been drinking it."

"No, thanks." But Nicholas sat down. "I suppose she takes this very hard."

"Mollie's death? Yes, they were very attached to one another."

"I know. I suppose the police haven't found out anything about it yet?"

"Not that I know of."

"They came round to see me last night, you know." The young man sounded more earnest than at any other time that Andrew had seen him. "And among other things they asked me if I'd a typewriter. I have, and they wanted me to type a few lines on it and they took the specimen away. I suppose you know why they did that."

"No," Andrew lied.

Nicholas looked at him sceptically. "I should have thought you would. It's that that I want to talk to Constance about. Possibly I ought to have done it before, but it's too late to worry about that now." He looked gloomily towards the window, through which the branches of the walnut tree could be seen tossing in the wind. "A foul morning," he muttered.

"How's your boil?" Andrew asked, just to keep the conversation going until Constance appeared.

"Oh, a bit better, thanks."

"Nasty things, boils."

"Yes, pretty painful."

"In the old days, before penicillin, they could lead to blood poisoning and kill you." Somehow it seemed inevitable to return to the subject of death.

"So I believe," Nicholas said.

The conversation did not seem to be getting anywhere. Whatever it was that had brought Nicholas, he plainly intended to keep it to himself until he could talk to Constance. Andrew gave up the attempt to converse, and happening to look down, noticed that he was waggling his toes in his socks. It was not very dignified. He was glad when he heard Constance coming down the stairs.

She had put on a light brown skirt and a dark-brown pullover and, as always, looked neat and self-contained. Nicholas stood up and gave her a kiss on each cheek.

"I'm sorry I'm so early," he said again, "but I've got people coming to look at the house and I've got to get home. They came to see it yesterday afternoon and they're coming again today with a surveyor. They say they're looking for a house to turn into a home for handicapped children. If the poor things are sufficiently handicapped, perhaps they won't realize how awful it is—Oh, Constance, I'm sorry, I didn't mean to talk nonsense like that. You can't be interested in my affairs at the moment, and anyway, I don't suppose the sale will come to anything. But there's something I've got to talk to you about."

"About a letter?" she inquired calmly.

She sat down and Nicholas sat down again.

"How did you guess?" he asked.

"But is it about a letter?"

"Yes." He looked dismayed at her foreknowledge of what he had come to say. "But how did you know?"

"It's about Mollie?"

"Yes. But until this thing happened to her, I didn't mean to say anything about it. It was rather a horrible letter."

"Have you brought it with you?"

"No, I destroyed it."

"But can you remember what was in it?" Her gaze on his face was interested but detached. There was more anxiety in her voice than in her expression.

"More or less," he answered. "It was odd, it didn't seem to have been written to me. It said something like 'I know all about what you did with Mrs. Ryan's last will and you'd better pay up. A thousand pounds. Cash. Get it ready and keep it till I write again to tell you where to put it.' "

"Ah yes," Constance said, "that's more or less what I expected."

"Do you mean you've had other letters like it?" he asked quickly.

"Not exactly like it, but there's a certain resemblance." Her tone was dry.

"Of course you know what Mollie did with that will," he said.

"Yes, I do, but I wasn't sure whether or not you did."

"It was only a guess till that letter came. I thought from the first Mollie must have destroyed the will, simply because she had the best opportunity to do it and the best motive. I admit it didn't seem like what I knew of her, but people are always doing things that strike one as out of character. I didn't really know her very well."

"Why didn't you accuse her of it and try to get the money that ought to have been yours?"

He stirred uneasily in his chair. "I don't quite know, Constance. I suppose it was because it seemed only fair to me that she should have it after the way she'd looked after my aunt. And what with death duties and income tax, added to what I've got already, it wouldn't have made so much difference to me. And I did get the house, which will sell sooner or later. Perhaps these people who are coming today will buy it. The land alone is worth a good deal. I've arranged for a firm of landscape gardeners to come in later today to start getting the place back into order again. But I suppose the real reason I didn't do anything is that I hate a fuss. There'd have been all sorts of arguments with lawyers, and perhaps it would have meant going to court, and in the end I might not have been able to prove anything. After all, my aunt could have destroyed that last will herself. We know she tore up some papers just before she died. Then that letter put me off altogether. Blackmail's a horrible thing."

"When did you get it?" Andrew asked.

"On Tuesday."

"And who do you think sent it?"

The young man shrugged his shoulders. "My bet is on Lorna Grace, the district nurse. But it could have been Pegler. The two of them say they witnessed a will, but I'm not even absolutely certain they did. They're the only people who ever saw it."

"I thought they claimed not to have read it," Andrew said.

"It would be in the interest of at least one of them to say that, wouldn't it? I mean, the one who'd seen the possibility of blackmail."

"I wonder then why they waited so long to try that. Mrs. Ryan's been dead a good while."

"I don't know. Perhaps this person suddenly needed money. And I don't know why the letter came to me, or how you knew about it, Constance."

"We won't go into that," she said. "Another time, perhaps, but not just now. Thank you for telling me about it, anyway. Have you told the police about it?"

"No."

"Are you going to?"

"I don't know. Do you think I should?"

"I think it might be best."

"Even though it means I'll have to explain what I guessed about Mollie and the will?"

"It can't hurt her now."

"Would it hurt you?"

She looked surprised for a moment, then she said, "Oh, you mean might it affect my inheriting anything under her will because the money wasn't really hers? But don't you know she left everything she'd got to you? Did you really not know that?"

Andrew saw a slow flush spread over the young man's face. He looked at Constance with what seemed to Andrew to be genuine disbelief.

"No, I didn't know that," he said in a low tone. Then all of a sudden his dark eyes flamed with rage. He sprang to his feet. "And that gives me a motive for murdering her! You believe I knew it. And murder's so much easier than a legal action. And cheaper too. This way I get my money without having to pay a single lawyer. Or are you going to contest the will, Constance? Because if you are, I warn you, I'll fight you."

"No, I shan't contest it," she said.

Her voice was extremely weary now. Andrew, remembering that she had probably not slept all night, wished that Nicholas would leave.

That seemed to be his intention, for he strode to the door. But there he paused.

"Somehow I'll get it out of you how you knew about the letter," he said. "It seems to me bloody strange. You say there have been other letters. All right, sooner or later you'll tell me about them. Goodbye."

"Goodbye, Nicholas. And I hope you manage to sell your house today."

He went out, letting the front door slam behind him.

She leant back in her chair and closed her eyes. Suddenly Andrew noticed that she was trembling. The interview had shaken her far more than she had allowed herself to show at the time.

He stayed silent for a little while, then he said quietly, "Do you still believe he's the murderer your letter was meant for?"

He saw that it was an effort for her to open her eyes and let her gaze meet his.

"It's probable, isn't it?" she said. "It might even be the real reason he came this morning. Like us, he may have guessed the letters had been muddled up and he wanted to know if I'd seen the one he may have been expecting. From the way it was worded, we know it wasn't the first the blackmailer sent to his victim."

"But didn't we agree Nicholas couldn't have murdered Mollie, or at least, as the Eckersalls said, that if he had he wouldn't have taken the awful risk of driving off in broad daylight with her body in his car when he'd a fine big garden in which to bury it safely?"

"Aren't you forgetting the landscape gardeners, Andrew? He'd arranged for them to come today to get to work on clearing up the place, so he couldn't bury her in the garden. And he'd got people coming to look over the house in the afternoon, so he'd got to get her out of the way in a hurry. It's true he could have hidden her in the boot of his car and waited for darkness to get rid of her, but he couldn't have driven along that lane by the stream without lights, and that would have been as conspicuous as doing it by daylight. And the question remains: whom besides Mollie may he have murdered? Who was our letter really about? At the moment I'm inclined to put my money on Mike Wakeham."

Chapter Seven

Andrew suddenly became aware that he had still not put on his slippers. Because he did not know how to respond to Constance, it seemed to him a good thing to go upstairs and put them on. Muttering that he would be back in a moment, he went upstairs. But then he changed his mind and, instead of putting on slippers, put on shoes, for he had just had an idea that presently he would go out and talk to Naomi.

Then it occurred to him that he ought to make his bed. Constance was hardly in a state to cope with domestic matters. He made his bed neatly, looked round the room to make sure that it was tidy and with a certain sense of reluctance went downstairs again. He did not really want to go on talking about murder. He thought of his own flat and how peaceful it was there, working on his notes of the life of Robert Hooke. He was very fond of Constance, but all the same it would have been very pleasant to be at home.

He found her sitting where he had left her.

"I've been thinking," she said as he came in, "I may be quite wrong about Mike Wakeham. For all I know, Nicholas may not even have been here when he disappeared. I'm not sure of the exact day it happened, of course, only that it was about three weeks ago. The first we knew of it was when Naomi came round and poured it all out to Mollie, how he'd gone off with some woman and she couldn't stand it any longer and was going to divorce him. But I suppose he'd disappeared at least a day or two before she did that."

"She's rather changed her story since then about what she thinks happened to him," Andrew said. "She seems to favour the idea that he's been murdered, though certainly not in Lindleham, in the service of MI5 or by drug smugglers. You still believe our murderer here is Nicholas, do you?"

"Don't you?"

"Because he got the letter meant for Mollie and the letter she got having been meant for him? But if you've given up the idea that his victim was Mike Wakeham, who else could it have been? Old Eckersall? He's probably safe in Fiji. Anyway, what had Nicholas against him? Colin? Had Nicholas anything against Colin? I'd an impression they were on rather good terms."

"I've been thinking about that too," Constance said. "The victim may not have been anyone from Lindleham. Nicholas might have brought someone down here, possibly someone who for some reason he hated or feared. We don't really know anything about his life in London. We know he's got money, but not much about where it comes from. It may be from something fairly disreputable, which he wanted to get out of when he inherited the house—oh, I know I'm being fanciful. All the same, it could be something like that, couldn't it?"

"Naomi claims to believe her husband may have been murdered by drug smugglers," Andrew said, "and you've changed it round, saying that some drug smuggler may have been murdered by Nicholas."

She gave a despondent little smile. "You make it sound so ridiculous. I think you always had a knack of doing that when I had extravagant ideas. It was probably very good for me. Let's go back to Mike Wakeham."

"But you're still convinced Nicholas is the murderer. I'm sorry about that. I rather like him."

"So many murderers are said to have been likeable."

"And his motive, I suppose, was that he was Naomi's lover. Yet he didn't speak of her as if he was in love with her, so much so that he'd commit murder for her sake."

"That could have been cunning."

"True. But what do we do if he has an alibi for the time of Wakeham's disappearance? Change the murderer or change the victim?"

"We might leave that, I think, till we know whether or not he's got an alibi." She stood up. "I'm going to call on the Gleesons."

"Why the Gleesons?"

"Because they know Nicholas much better than I do, and their cottage is almost opposite the gates of Lindleham House. They may have seen him come and go at that time. Of course, if they didn't see him it doesn't necessarily mean he wasn't there. He might have been deliberately making himself inconspicuous."

"Mrs. Grainger, the housekeeper, would know whether or not he was there."

"But we can hardly go and question her about it, can we? Not at the moment, anyway, when he's in the house and showing his prospective purchasers round it. No, I'm going to the Gleesons'. As it's Saturday, I think Jim will be there as well as Leslie. Do you want to come with me?"

"I was thinking of going to talk to Naomi. I want to ask her if the man she saw in the grey Vauxhall could have been the man called Banks who used to live in the Gleesons' cottage."

"What's the point? You know you can't rely on anything Naomi tells you. Why not come with me?"

"If you want me to."

He stood up too.

"Better get a coat," she said. "It looks as if it might start raining at any time."

It had not started raining as they set out, but dark masses of cloud were pushing their way across the sky and the treetops bowed and complained in the wind. It was much colder than it had been the day before. When Constance rang the bell at the Gleesons' front door there was no answer. She rang it twice more and the sound of it ringing inside the cottage was clearly audible, but still no one came to the door.

"They're out," Constance said. "We may as well go home."

As she said it the first scattered drops of a shower began to fall. At the same time Andrew became aware that he could hear voices coming from somewhere near, raised, angry voices. It seemed to him that they were coming from behind the cottage.

"I believe they're out at the back," he said. "Do you want to go round and see if they're there?"

Constance listened for a moment, then nodded and led the way along the paved path that skirted the cottage to the garden at the back of it. There they found Jim and Leslie Gleeson facing each other across the rose bed that the Eckersalls had described to Andrew. They were shouting at each other, unconscious of the appearance of Constance and Andrew round the corner of the cottage, and disputing about a big hole that had been dug in the rose bed. Since Gleeson had a spade in his hand, it seemed likely that it was he who had done the digging.

"Stop it, stop it!" Leslie shouted at him. "Are you mad? Have you gone out of your mind?"

"I'm only doing what you wanted me to do!" he shouted back at her. "You weren't going to give me any peace till I'd done it."

Though they were both shouting the wind had the effect of muting their voices.

Jim's face was red from anger and from the exertion of digging. Leslie's had a painful pallor.

"I didn't mean it!" she yelled, her words almost carried away by the wind. "Haven't I been telling you I didn't mean it?"

"You did mean it, you meant every bloody word of it, and there's only one way to prove to you what a crazy bitch you are and that's to dig the whole place up and show you there's nothing here but some miserable roses."

"But it's only what the Eckersalls said about its being the wrong time to plant roses, and I didn't mean—"

"Bloody Eckersalls!" he roared. "Snooping, gossiping old bitches, putting crazy ideas in your head. You think that son of yours is buried down here and I'm going to go on digging the whole place up till you can see there's nothing here but roses. If I tell you he isn't here you won't believe a word of it, you'll go on giving me those queer looks you've been giving me lately and saying why did I suddenly have to dig the place over—"

"Jim, Jim!" she shrieked at him. "I just couldn't understand why you dug it up when you'd hurt your back. And you oughtn't to be digging now. It'll only make your back worse."

"My back's giving me hell, let me tell you! But I'm going to dig the place up and chuck the roses away and then you can do what you like with the big hole outside your window. I'll dig it up, but I'm damned if I'll fill it in again. I'll leave it as it is to remind you that you can just go so far and no farther, telling your husband he's a murderer."

Her temper seemed suddenly to go completely out of control. "Murderer, murderer! Go on, dig, dig! I'll stand and watch you! You think if you shout enough and talk about your back and curse me, I'll go away and you won't have to finish digging. You won't have to go as deep down as a grave. Go on— why have you stopped digging?"

For a moment he seemed taken aback, then grasping his spade, he stepped down into the hole and started digging with wild energy, tossing earth out to right and left of it.

Constance chose that moment to walk forward.

"Leslie, I'm afraid we heard most of that," she said. "We tried ringing at the front door, but didn't get any answer, then we heard your voices from round here and there was something we wanted to ask you, so we came looking for you. We weren't snooping, but I gather you've been listening to the Eckersalls, and now Jim's digging up your flower bed to prove he didn't bury poor little Colin there. But you don't really believe he did, do you?"

As she spoke heavier rain began to fall. Jim Gleeson straightened up, thrusting his spade into the soil, letting go of it and leaving it standing there. He stepped out of the hole.

"She believes it all right," he said. "She's believed I did him in ever since that brat ran away. And I'm tired of hearing him called poor little Colin. He knew what he was doing, or he thought he knew. He was out to make as much trouble as he could for everyone. If he's had to pay a worse price for it than he reckoned, it's his own bloody fault."

Leslie, who was wearing only jeans and a sweater, gave a shiver as the rain, or it might have been the meaning of her husband's words, chilled even the heat of her anger.

"Come inside out of the rain," she said. "If it gets any worse that bed will soon be mud and Jim won't be able to dig anyway. I've been telling him not to, but he won't listen to me."

She pushed open the French window behind her that led straight into the sitting room. With its low, beamed ceiling, the low, heavy clouds in the sky and the rain which was now falling in a torrent, it was very dark. The bowl of lilac that had stood in the great open hearth when Andrew had last been here was still where it had been, but the flowers were fading.

Gleeson followed the others in, pausing in the doorway to kick off the gum boots he was wearing.

"She told me not to, but all the same she wanted me to do it," he said. Surprisingly, he put an arm round Leslie's shoulders and drew her against him. "And I'll finish the job presently. That'll be the best thing for both of us. But I'm afraid we both rather lost our heads about it. Sorry, love."

She resisted him for a moment, then let him hold her.

"Yes, we've both been stupid," she said. "It's the strain. You don't know how awful it is, Constance. One completely loses one's sense of proportion. I told Jim what the Eckersalls said about the roses and he thought I meant—well, perhaps I did mean it, but only for a moment. I never expected him to rush out and start digging up the bed."

"Look, let's stop talking about it," he said. He let her go as if his mood of affection had soon faded. "I know I planted those roses at the wrong time. It was simply because they were given to me. A chap in the office told me he'd been digging some of his up and was going to throw them away and plant something else, so I said why not give them to me, I'll see if they'll go in an empty bed we've got. That's all there was to it. You said there was something you wanted to ask us, Constance."

They had all found places to sit down except Gleeson, who had remained standing just inside the French window, which he had not closed behind him. Rain was splashing on to the doorstep and on to his feet, but he took no notice of it. It made him look as if he did not expect his visitors to stay long. Andrew remembered how he had given the same impression the last time that they had met. He also remembered that on that occasion he had thought that there was something brutal about the man's heavily handsome features and had wondered what a child might be driven to do who was at his mercy.

"I wanted to ask you something about Mike Wakeham," Constance said. "Do you know exactly when he disappeared?"

"Mike?" Leslie said, surprised. "Exactly when? What day of the week, d'you mean?"

"Yes, it was about three weeks ago, wasn't it?" Constance answered. "But I wondered if you could pinpoint it a little more accurately."

"Why?" Gleeson asked harshly.

"It would be a bit complicated to explain," Constance said, putting on a vagueness that was not like her. "But do you remember?"

Leslie frowned in thought, then shook her head.

"I know it happened a week or so after Colin went missing," she said, "and really that was all I could think of at the time. Naomi came here one day and told me how Mike had disappeared and I don't think I was very kind to her. I thought the obvious thing was for her to ditch him as soon as she could. He was no good. But I was so obsessed with our trouble about Colin that I wasn't as sympathetic as I might have been. But wait a minute!" She took her head in her hands, trying to concentrate. "Colin disappeared four weeks ago tomorrow, which was a Sunday, and the next Sunday I went to church. I don't often go, but that day I wanted to, and it was when I got home that Naomi came in and told me about Mike. But of course that wasn't the day he'd gone. I think it was on the Friday before. He'd left for work as usual on the Friday morning and simply hadn't come back for the weekend. Yes, I think it was that Friday, which makes it three weeks ago yesterday. Is that what you wanted to know?"

"Yes, but I wonder if you can tell me something else," Constance said. "Do you know if Nicholas was here at the time?"

"Now what are you getting at?" Gleeson demanded. "Are you trying to connect Nicholas with Mike's disappearance?"

"I said it would be a bit complicated to explain," Constance said coolly. "Don't answer if you don't feel like it."

"I don't feel like it," Gleeson said. "I don't like getting mixed up in things I don't understand."

"I understand it's got something to do with Mollie," Leslie said. "It has, hasn't it, though I can't see how. And I'd help if I could. Let me think. No, Nicholas wasn't here that weekend. When I was starting out for church I met Mrs. Grainger leaving for the village too and I gave her a lift and she told me Nicholas would be coming down the next weekend to try to get the agents in Maddingleigh to do something active about selling the house. She said when he did sell it she was going to live with a sister in Nottingham, and though she'd be sorry to leave after so many years, she was hoping it would be soon, because it was very unsettling not knowing how long she was going to stay on. So he wasn't here the weekend Mike went away."

"Does that satisfy you?" Gleeson asked, looking at Constance with a mixture of curiosity and hostility. "I wish I knew what you're getting at."

"Nothing, if Nicholas wasn't here," Constance answered. "Just an idea I had that seems not to have been a very good one."

"I know how it is," Leslie said. "When something happens like Mollie's death or Colin's disappearance, you start thinking the most unlikely, disconnected things, because it seems to you that you must be able to make sense of it if only you try hard enough. You can't be just left groping forever in a horrible cloud that won't go away. I know one gets desperate and muddled and unreasonable."

"The rain's stopping," Gleeson said, turning to look out into the garden. "I'm going out to finish the digging." He started struggling back into his gum boots.

Leslie leapt from her chair. "Don't! Don't do it! Didn't I tell you I knew it was all nonsense about the roses and that he isn't there?"

"By this evening you'll be sure again that he is, if I haven't given you proof positive that he isn't."

"I tell you, stop it! You'll hurt your back."

"To hell with my back. A lot you care about it."

He strode out into the rain, which now was falling only thinly. As he stepped down into the hole in the flower bed Leslie dashed out after him, imploring him to forget that she had ever dreamt that her child might be buried there. Constance met Andrew's eyes, gave him a little signal with her head that it was time for them to leave the cottage, and the two of them let themselves out by the front door and started along the lane.

"So much for my theory," Constance said. "Nicholas wasn't here. That seems pretty definite."

"I never felt too happy about the idea," Andrew admitted. "But d'you know, I've a feeling there's some obvious fact we haven't spotted that might tell us all we need to know. You know how it is in our field when one's got a hunch that something would fit but one hasn't got quite the experimental evidence to clinch it. Well, that's how I'm feeling now."

But he was quite at sea when he tried to think what the missing fact might be. As they walked back to Cherry Tree

Cottage he would have liked to suggest to Constance that the two of them should get into her car and drive a good distance away from Lindleham till they found a nice pub in some peaceful spot and there have a good lunch with a bottle of wine and talk once more about the interests that they had shared in the old days and let the subject of murder rest.

But of course it would be shockingly insensitive to make any such suggestion, and anyway, peaceful spots could be deceptive. What could have looked more peaceful than Lindleham during the past day or two before the wind had got up and the heavy shower of rain had turned the ditches on each side of the lane into muddy little rivers? If he and Constance were to arrive for their lunch in some spot softly encircled by the downs, remote and quiet, with larks singing in the sky above, it might turn out that the local police were trying to arrest a bank robber who had taken refuge there and was holding the landlord of the inn and his wife and family as hostages. Anything was possible these days.

He thought of the time when it had been a matter of pride to the Briton that our police went unarmed, and then of the pictures of them so often seen now on television armed to the teeth with rifles and revolvers. Alas, for the old days!

> *With weeping and with laughter*
> *Still is the story told*
> *How well Horatius kept the bridge*
> *In the brave days of old...*

That miserable Horatius was getting mixed up with his thoughts again. Not that he could imagine why anyone should weep or laugh at that particular story. There was nothing very funny about it, and as the man had been successful, there was nothing to weep over either. And he had never believed that those old days had been any more brave than the frightened days of today. Under the surface very little changed. If terrorism and violent crime were on the increase and if traffic accidents were as lethal as a mediaeval plague, at least tuberculosis and many other diseases had been conquered, and who knew, a cure even for cancer might be just round the corner. On the whole, given a choice, he would prefer to live in the world of today rather than those as comparatively recent as his own childhood.

A car was coming along the lane from the crossroads. It was a police car, and as Constance and Andrew were just about to enter the cottage, it stopped at the gate. Superintendent Stonor and Sergeant Southby got out of it.

Coming up the path towards the door, the superintendent said in a sombre tone, "Good morning."

It was less a greeting than a mere announcement of his presence, in case there should be any doubt about the matter.

At the sound of it a quick look of apprehension came into Constance's eyes, but she did not ask him there on the doorstep what had brought him.

"Come in," she said, and opened the door and led the way in.

In the hall, without speaking, the men took off their raincoats and Constance took them and hung them up on pegs on the wall, then led the way into the sitting room.

"Sit down," she said, and herself sat down on a straight-backed chair as if she felt it would give her more support than any of the more comfortable chairs when the blow came which she had certainly guessed, from the looks on the faces of the two men, was about to fall. As before, Andrew had the feeling that Stonor was glad to see him there. He seemed to be at a loss how to deal with the small, fragile yet powerful woman facing him.

Sitting down, he said, "I'm bringing you more bad news, Professor."

"So I supposed," Constance said.

"Yes, I—I imagined you would." He spoke hesitantly. "I thought you should hear it from us, and then perhaps you can answer some questions I would like to ask you."

"Please go on," she said.

"This morning, at nine o'clock, when a Mrs. Jolson, who is Dr. Pegler's daily maid, arrived at his house as usual," he said, "she found Dr. Pegler dead. He was lying on the floor beside his desk in a room that he appears to have used as an office. He had been stabbed several times with some long, narrow-bladed knife, which had been removed. His wounds were very like your sister's. He bled very heavily. In fact, it may have been the bleeding that killed him, rather than any of the stab wounds." He paused; then as Constance only stared at him as if it were totally beyond her to say anything, he added, "There's something else I should tell you. We have positive proof that he was your blackmailer."

❋ ❋ ❋

A long sigh came from Constance. "You've proof, you say."

"The simplest proof," Stonor answered. "He'd a typewriter in his office and the letter you gave us was certainly typed on it."

"Then he wasn't a very clever little man, was he?" she said. "He should have stuck to cricket. And now he's dead. When did it happen?"

"The forensic people have put it at some time between nine o'clock yesterday evening and midnight."

"I can't help feeling sorry for him," she said. "I suppose it was someone else he tried to blackmail who killed him."

"It seems probable."

"I know who that may have been."

That seemed to Andrew to be going a little far, and Stonor's eyebrows went up, as if he did not believe her.

"How's that?" he asked.

"I know who got the letter that was meant for my sister concerning her destruction of Mrs. Ryan's will," she answered. "It was Nicholas Ryan. He told me so himself. And that makes it likely, doesn't it, that the letter that came here concerning a murder was meant for him. That seems clear enough to me. The only question is: whom did he murder?"

"Quite a question," Stonor remarked.

"I thought myself it might be Mr. Wakeham," she said. "You know he's disappeared? But I was told this morning Nicholas wasn't here when that happened."

He nodded. "That's right. We've been doing some checking up on it, and Mr. Wakeham seems to have vanished off the face of the earth. His former employers haven't heard of him for about three months, though he'd told no one here he'd left them. Apparently he kept up a show of being in a job when he'd been sacked the first time he gave himself some leave without permission. He left Maddingleigh as usual on Friday morning three weeks ago as if he was going to their office, and he hasn't been seen since. But it seems that Mr. Ryan, whom you suspect of murder, was in Paris at that time. That's been checked very carefully and there's no question of it. So if it was he who killed Dr. Pegler last night because he was tired of being blackmailed, and who probably killed your sister because he thought she knew too much, we've still got to find another victim."

"It couldn't be Colin," Constance said thoughtfully, glancing at Andrew as if she wanted support from him. "Nicholas had nothing against the child."

"Child murderers sometimes have nothing against their victims," Stonor said. "In their perverse way they some-times have a sort of love for them. We just caught up with one yesterday. We'd found a boy's body in the river beyond Maddingleigh some days ago and we thought it might be Colin Gleeson and we got Mr. and Mrs. Gleeson to come along and identify him. A mistake. It wasn't Colin. We were very sorry to have put his mother through such an ordeal. It was the son of a couple who live in Maddingleigh, who'd reported the boy missing a week ago and who were as desperate about it, poor people, as she is. But at least we've got the murderer. His wife suddenly couldn't stand things any longer and came in to us and broke down and told us all she knew and showed us some of the boy's clothes which she'd managed to get hold of and hide from her husband to prove her story. And Banks, the murderer, has confessed to that killing and to two others in other parts of the country that hadn't been solved. But he absolutely denies having laid a finger on Colin Gleeson. He may or may not be telling the truth. We don't know yet."

"Banks!" Constance exclaimed. "Isn't that the name of the man who used to live in the cottage the Gleesons have now and who was sent to prison for receiving stolen scrap iron? And his wife was an alcoholic, and no wonder, if she knew what kind of man he was. And they'd a grey Vauxhall, so I've been told. Do you know about the grey Vauxhall that was seen in the lane yesterday morning, Mr. Stonor?"

He shook his head.

"Mrs. Wakeham told us about it," she said. "She'd been in Clareham to do some shopping and have coffee with some people there, and on her way back she passed my sister at the crossroads, then saw a grey Vauxhall with a man in it parked near the Eckersalls' gate. She didn't pay it much attention at the time and she couldn't describe the man, she just happened to notice the kind of car it was. Has Banks still got a grey Vauxhall?"

"He has, but it wasn't his car here yesterday morning," the superintendent answered. "We'd already pulled him in by then."

"Then probably it had nothing to do with my sister's death. It was just someone who'd lost his way."

He nodded. "Probably. But we'll look into it."

Andrew noticed that Sergeant Southby had rapidly produced a notebook and was writing in it.

"Did Mrs. Wakeham tell you nothing about the car when you questioned her yesterday?" Andrew asked.

"No."

"I suppose she hadn't realized its possible importance, even if it didn't belong to Banks. But I've just thought of something. Dr. Pegler told us that for a time when his wife left him he took to drinking very heavily. But he said that even after drinking a bottle of whisky he'd be stone-cold sober. That was his phrase. And he said that when he had to go out on a call in the evening he was sure his patients noticed nothing the matter with him. And I think it somehow stuck in my mind that a doctor is someone who sometimes has to go out late at night and that on one of those trips he might have seen something... Well, if you're sure he was the blackmailer, we know he did, he saw a body being buried. But why did his victim wait till last night to murder him? Why didn't he do it as soon as the blackmail started?"

"Possibly because he didn't find out till some time in the last few days who his blackmailer was," Stonor said.

"And there's another thing," Andrew went on. "If Pegler saw a body being buried on one of his late calls, doesn't it mean that if you can trace from his records what calls he made during the relevant time, you'll at least know what routes he followed on those occasions and be able to check what he might have been able to see from the various roads he may have driven along?"

"That's an interesting thought," Stonor said, but something in his tone gave Andrew the feeling that he had already thought of it himself.

Constance gave a sharp little ironic smile.

"Then how we were wasting our time this morning," she said. "That rose bed behind the Gleesons' cottage wouldn't have been visible from the lane in daylight, let alone in David's headlights."

"A rose bed?" Stonor said, tilting his head slightly in a request for an explanation of what she meant.

"Yes, we've been watching a man digging up a rose bed, looking for a body," Constance replied.

She told him what she and Andrew had done that morning, of how they had found Jim Gleeson digging up the rose bed at the back of the cottage and of the quarrel that he and Leslie had been having about it when she and Andrew had arrived. She said she believed it had been the Eckersall sisters who had put it into Leslie's head that her son's body might be there, but that it had been obvious enough, she thought, even before Jim Gleeson had resumed his digging after the rain had lessened, that nobody, even a child, could be buried there.

A little to Andrew's surprise, Stonor showed a deep interest in the story.

"Yes," he said thoughtfully as Constance ended it. "Yes, I see. Quite so. Exactly. Of course nothing to be found there. All the same, very interesting..." He seemed to be muttering almost meaninglessly to himself. "A very valuable piece of information. It's always rewarding to deal with intelligent people. Thank you."

He got to his feet and looked as if he were in a hurry to be gone. The sergeant tucked his notebook into a pocket and got up too.

"I'm sorry we've nothing to tell you yet about your sister," the superintendent said. "As soon as we have, of course we'll be in touch. And concerning Pegler..." He paused. "You know, he'd just got himself an aquarium full of some kind of tropical fish. Quite an expensive sort of thing. Mrs. Jolson said he was crazy about it. He didn't expect to die, though a blackmailer should always remember he's at risk. Thank you for your help. Goodbye."

Andrew saw the two detectives out.

When he came back into the sitting room Constance exploded. "Now what in hell did he mean by that, Andrew? 'A very valuable piece of information...' About that rose bed. Hadn't I just explained to him that it meant nothing at all?"

"He's nobody's fool," Andrew said. "And he knows much more about this kind of thing than you or I do. What you said may have given him some idea. Shall we have a drink?"

She nodded without answering and sat staring broodingly before her.

"Valuable information!" she muttered. "And our help! What nonsense!"

Andrew poured out sherry for them both.

"Constance, have you thought at all about what you're going to do when all this is over?" he asked. "This house, along with Mollie's money, will go to Ryan, won't it?"

It took her a moment to come back from some distance to which her thoughts had briefly departed. She looked confused as if she were still thinking of something else.

"I suppose it will, unless they get proof that he's the murderer," she said. "You can't benefit from a crime you've committed, can you? Financially, I mean. No, I haven't really started to think about the future yet. I shan't stay here, I know that much. London's my natural habitat. I'll take a small flat somewhere and perhaps I'll copy you and settle down to writing somebody's life. Malpighi's, for instance."

Malpighi was a seventeenth-century botanist who had explained the structure of a plant stem. Andrew felt some doubt whether that possible life would progress much farther than the life of Robert Hooke with which he had been engaged for the last few years, but with Constance you never knew. If she decided to apply her formidable mental energy to the task, it might prosper in a way that would put his own efforts to shame.

"Of course, you've got your pension," he said. "It's not wealth, but you should be able to manage."

"Oh yes, I shan't be in want."

The door knocker sounded.

"I'll see who that is," Andrew said, put down his glass of sherry and went to open the door.

A young woman stood there whom he was sure that he had never seen before, yet he had a curious feeling that there was something familiar about her. He thought that she was about thirty-five. She was almost as tall as he was and wide-shouldered, with narrow hips and long legs in black jeans and she was wearing a black nylon windcheater, zipped up to her throat. She had short brown hair that clustered round her face in curls and was spattered with raindrops. There was something boyish about her build and she was handsome in a hard-featured way.

The rain had almost stopped, but the paved path behind her was dotted with puddles in which small splashes showed that the shower was not quite over.

She looked as if his appearance took her aback.

"Oh, I didn't know—" she said uncertainly. "Are you the police?"

"No, I'm a friend of Professor Camm's," he answered. "I'm staying with her."

"I'm Carolyn Pegler," she said. "Is Constance in? Can I see her?"

"Yes, come in." He assumed that Constance would be accessible to this woman, if not to many other people. He remembered now where he had seen her. It had been in the photograph that Leslie Gleeson had shown him, a photograph taken just after he had scored a century against the formidable might of Little Millpen. "My name's Basnett."

"Ah, I've heard of you from Constance," she said. She stepped inside. "Have the police been here?"

"Yes, and told us about your husband's death. May I say how sorry—"

"Don't, don't!" she interrupted, to his relief, for he had not the least idea how one should express sympathy about the death of her husband to a woman who had recently left him, a man, moreover, who the police were completely sure was a blackmailer. "Of course it's awful—I mean, murder, all those stab wounds, horrible. But he had it coming to him, as I warned him before I left." She went into the sitting room. "Hallo, Constance," she said. "We've all got our troubles, haven't we? I've heard about Mollie—I'm so sorry—and I understand you've heard about David. I've just been saying to Professor Basnett that David had it coming to him. But now it's happened, I can't take it in. I've a feeling I'm to blame. I am, you know, because I knew what he was doing. It was why I left him. Yes, thank you," she added to Andrew, who was offering her a drink. "Gin and tonic, please."

Constance, who had not stood up when the other woman entered, was giving her a long and penetrating stare.

"So you aren't a victim," she said.

"A victim—of what?" Carolyn Pegler asked. "Yes, I'm a victim of my own stupidity and cowardice. I couldn't face all the trouble there'd be if I let on to anyone what David was doing, or why he was doing it, so I just went away."

She sat down and accepted the drink that Andrew had poured out for her.

"But you're alive," Constance said. "It appears we've a murderer loose in our midst, but we don't know who he's murdered. And I just wondered, since you'd disappeared, if it might perhaps be you."

Carolyn gave a short laugh.

"Would you care to tell me what you're talking about?" she said. "I came here to tell you how bad I feel about Mollie because I've a feeling David was somehow involved in her death, but I didn't expect to be told I'm supposed to be dead myself."

"I didn't think that very seriously," Constance answered. "But I'm glad you've been eliminated from our list of suspect corpses. But d'you mean you've known for some time, Carolyn, that David was trying his hand at blackmail?"

Carolyn Pegler leant back in her chair, sipped her drink and said, "Yes, I saw a letter David wrote to Mollie. He'd just typed it and it was lying on his desk and I picked it up and read it. It said he'd known for a long time that she'd destroyed Mrs. Ryan's last will and that now he needed money and she'd got to pay for his silence. But it wasn't signed and the money was to be sent in cash to an accommodation address in London. I tore the letter up and we had a flaming row and I told him that if he ever tried to do such a thing again I'd go and tell Mollie myself who'd written it and if she wanted she could go to the police. And he laughed and said she'd never believe me. If she suspected anyone in particular it would be Lorna Grace, because she was the other witness of the will. Actually he was blind drunk at the time and I couldn't get him to talk sense. He used to get through a bottle of whisky every evening and he was always convinced no one could tell he wasn't sober. So I left him." She gave a little shudder. "I'd been on the edge of doing it for some time because of his drinking and he knew it, and I believe that's why he took to blackmail. He thought if he could give me more money I'd stay. But money had nothing to do with it. I was bored, I didn't love him, I didn't trust him and I like money, but not if it's come by that way."

"Do you know anything about his having seen someone burying a body?" Constance asked. "Do you know of anyone besides Mollie whom he was trying to blackmail?"

Carolyn's eyebrows went up in surprise. They were very thin eyebrows that looked as if they had been drawn with pencil on her pale, hard face.

"No," she said, "I don't know anything about that. But what happened? I don't understand."

"You see, someone—I didn't know it was David then—sent Mollie a letter saying he'd seen her burying a body," Constance said. "He demanded money. And Nicholas Ryan got a letter accusing him of destroying Mrs. Ryan's will and demanding a thousand pounds, but the way that letter was worded it seemed obvious it was meant for Mollie. So it's fairly certain, isn't it, that the letters got mixed up and got into the wrong envelopes?"

"And Nicholas is a murderer?" There was incredulity in Carolyn's voice. "Oh no!"

"We can't say that until we find a body, can we?" Constance said. "The *corpus delicti*."

"Which isn't me!"

"Just so. But did David ever say anything, drop a hint, tell you anything that sounded to you like half-drunk maundering, to suggest he'd found out something really dramatic about somebody?"

Carolyn frowned, her thin eyebrows almost meeting above her aquiline nose.

"No," she said. "But you know, the whole thing could have been purely imaginary."

"You mean he didn't really see anything?"

"Yes, it could have been a kind of delusion. He may have wanted so much to have power over someone because they'd committed some really serious crime, like murder, so that he could demand a great deal more than a thousand pounds, that he just made it all up."

"When he was drunk?"

"Yes."

"I don't think I believe that," Constance said. "Mollie's death wasn't imaginary. Nor was David's. Someone's got a secret which they'll commit murder to hide."

"But he was certainly drunk when he mixed up Mollie's letter with the one to Nicholas, wasn't he?" Carolyn said.

"I suppose so. And so we get back to Nicholas as a possible murderer. But the only person I think of whom he'd any motive for murdering is Mike Wakeham and the police have told us he was abroad when Mike disappeared."

"Why should he have murdered Mike?" Carolyn asked.

"It could have happened during a quarrel between them over Naomi. It might not actually have been Nicholas who started it. If Mike was jealous he could have been the one who began it, and it's even possible that Nicholas killed him by accident, defending himself when Mike attacked him. Mike was much the more violent of the two."

"Only, as you say, Nicholas happens to have been abroad at the time," Andrew reminded her. "And I can't believe he's Naomi's lover. There's something about the way he talks of her that doesn't fit. Of course, as you said, that could be just his cleverness, covering it up, but I believe the reason he's been down here so much recently, as you say he has, is simply that he wants to get that house sold."

"So you agree with Carolyn that David's idea that he saw Nicholas burying someone could be imaginary."

"I'd like to, but really I don't," Andrew said.

Carolyn finished her drink and stood up. "We don't seem able to help each other much, do we, Constance? I'm feeling even more confused than when I came. I wish I could get back to London. I've been lucky enough to get a job I think I'm going to like and I can't pretend I miss David. If only he'd died a natural death, or even been in an ordinary traffic accident, I shouldn't feel so bad about it. But murder's hard to take. Well, goodbye. I expect I'll have to stay around for at least a few days, if you should want to see me."

She went to the door and Andrew saw her out. Then he returned to the sitting room.

"A somewhat hard-boiled character," he said.

"Oh yes, she was always that," Constance said.

"Let me get you another drink."

She held out her glass for him to refill it.

As he brought it back to her she said, "I'm sorry I've got you into all this, Andrew. I know you hate it. But I'm so grateful to you for staying here. I can't think of anyone else I could have turned to."

"If you want me to be honest about it," he said as he sat down again, "I'll admit the situation is beginning to have a ghastly sort of fascination for me. I'm meeting such interesting people. A woman who would be perfectly happy if only her husband had died in his bed or in a head-on crash with a lorry. A couple who dig for a body in their rose bed. Two elderly ladies who believe that planting roses at the wrong time of year is indicative of criminal tendencies. A beautiful young woman who thinks her husband was murdered while working for MI5. An alcoholic doctor who writes anonymous letters and sees visions. No university department I ever had anything to do with could produce a collection like that, yet we're said to be a fairly eccentric gang."

"You've left out Nicholas," Constance said.

"So I have."

"You really don't think he murdered Mike, do you?"

"Unless he's faked his alibi, how could he?"

"Can't alibis be faked?"

"I'm sure they can, but the police seem fairly positive about this one."

"Suppose then it wasn't Mike."

He gave her a thoughtful look. She met his gaze with an unusual air of diffidence, as if she were putting forward some theory which she more than half expected him to tear to pieces.

"You really think it's possible he might have murdered Colin Gleeson?" he said.

She gave an abrupt shudder. "I know it doesn't seem possible. He's too normal. All the same, I wonder if it's possible to tell about a thing like that. Whenever some character like that man Banks the superintendent was telling us about gets arrested for assaulting and murdering children, half the people they know come forward to say what nice, ordinary sorts of chaps they are. I know Banks's wife found out the truth about him and at last couldn't stand it and went to the police, but Nicholas hasn't a wife. And he isn't really intimate with anyone here except perhaps Naomi, and you don't believe in that. So where are we? Now I ought to be doing something about lunch. Can you face bread and cheese again?"

Andrew felt the greatest reluctance to face bread and cheese. Although it was a normal lunch for him at home, he now felt a craving for something hot and sustaining, something like roast beef and Yorkshire pudding or steak-and-kidney pie. Only a little while ago, when a similar feeling had come to him, he had thought that it would be shockingly insensitive to suggest to Constance that they might go out together and enjoy a good meal. But now he was inclined to think, from her tone of voice, that perhaps bread and cheese were getting on her nerves too.

"I was wondering if there's a pub in Clareham where we might get a decent meal," he said. "It would save you trouble."

She showed signs of relief.

"There's the Swan, which isn't bad," she said, "and I'd love to get away from this house for a little while. Yes, let's go. Then I can pick up something in Smither's for the evening. Something frozen, if you don't mind. I don't feel much like cooking."

"Fine," he said. "It's stopped raining. Shall we walk?"

She agreed and went to fetch her coat. The two of them left the house together and started towards the gate.

But there they were checked. Just as they reached it Jean and Kate Eckersall emerged, almost running, from their own gate. The brown dog was leaping about behind them and uttering short, sharp barks, as if he had been infected by the excitement that seemed to have possessed his owners. They came hurrying towards Constance and Andrew. Their brown smocks blew out around them in the wind and their canvas shoes squelched in the mud of the lane.

"Oh, Constance, isn't it awful?" the one with the green socks, who Andrew was fairly sure by now was Jean, cried out, shouting against the wind. "It's terrible! We don't know how to face it. One ought to be able to stop a thing like that, but they won't listen to us. The police, you know. That superintendent we thought was so nice treated us as if we're fools. We said we'd get a lawyer, or an injunction, or something, but he just said not to worry, it wouldn't take any time at all and they'd put everything back very nicely and we needn't watch. Watch, my goodness! That's just what we're going to do, because God knows what damage they're going to do if we don't keep a lookout. And I'm sure we've some rights as citizens, but we don't know what they are, and he said something about having a warrant, so we can't really do anything. But we'll watch, oh yes, we'll watch!"

"But what are they going to do?" Constance asked.

"They're going to dig up poor little Timmie's grave," Jean bellowed as if she were speaking to Constance from a great distance. "They're going to desecrate it. And all because they think someone may have been buried under it while we were away in Scotland. I believe they think it's that child Colin, and of course, if it is it's terrible, monster though he was, and they've got to do their duty, but to dig up Timmie's grave—oh, Constance, we can't bear it!"

"We're going to tell Leslie about it," Kate shouted. "We think she ought to know."

"Oh, don't do that," Constance said quickly. "She's had enough to go through. She's had to look at murdered children who turned out not to be Colin and she's had to wait and hope and despair. Don't tell her anything till the police have finished what they're going to do."

"No, it's only fair to her to let her know what's happening," Jean answered. "She'll want to be there. Come along, Kate."

The two sisters set off briskly towards the Gleesons' cottage.

Watching them go with their smocks ballooning around them, Andrew suddenly exclaimed, "Constance, we've been the most awful fools!"

"I don't doubt it," she said, "but what's brought on this attack of self-doubt?"

"It's because of something I've only just thought of," he answered. "Those letters. We've been taking for granted, haven't we, that two letters got mixed up?"

"Yes. Don't you think so now? Have you any other explanation?"

"No, they got mixed up all right. But why have we been assuming that there were only two letters? Why didn't we think there could be three? If there were, you see, it explains a lot of things."

Chapter Eight

Constance and Andrew hardly talked on their way to the Swan in Clareham. Constance, who had a look of intense concentration on her face, was trying to work out for herself the implications of what he had said. When they were settled in the old, dark dining room of the pub, with its small windows, its thick ceiling beams and its smell of excellent cooking, she gave a nod and said, "I see. I think I see."

They were lucky that that day there was roast duckling on the menu with new potatoes and peas. They decided together on a carafe of red wine, whatever that might turn out to be, and before it sherry.

Waiting for their drinks to be brought, Andrew said, "I told you I had a hunch about the whole situation, the feeling that really I knew what had happened, but one of the puzzling things, of course, has been why the murderer waited until yesterday to kill Pegler. We know, from the wording of the letter Mollie got, that that wasn't the first letter he'd written to the murderer, telling him how and what to pay. So why didn't whoever it was get to work straightaway, unless it was simply because he didn't know who'd written the first letter? But if that was how it was, then something must have happened during the last few days which told him it was Pegler. And what did happen? One thing was that Pegler, when he was drunk and frantic because his wife had left him, muddled up at least two letters, one of which came to Mollie and one to Nicholas Ryan. But Pegler himself told us, that evening at the Gleesons', that there were some other letters he intended to write. He was going to write to various people thanking them for their contributions to the new cricket pavilion. And if one of those letters went by mistake to the man he was blackmailing, he could have recognized the typing as being the same as the original blackmail letter and understood at last whom it had come from."

"And decided to get rid of him," Constance said.

"Yes."

"But why did he have to get rid of Mollie?"

Their sherry had come and she was fingering the stem of the glass, gazing down at it as if it were a specimen that she was examining under a microscope and which of itself would tell her something that she needed to know.

"I think the chances are we'll never know the exact truth about that," Andrew said. "I've a rough idea of what it probably was, but unless they catch the murderer and he decides to talk, we may never be quite sure. I think Mollie decided she wanted a quiet talk with Pegler about that heart attack of yours. You said she was very worried about it and wanted you to see someone in London, and she may have hoped to be able to have a word about it with Pegler in his surgery. But he was particularly rushed that morning and she didn't have a chance to do it. So when she was put down at the crossroads by Miss Grace, she stood there, hesitating, thinking that perhaps she'd go to Pegler's house and wait for him there and hope she'd be able to have a talk with him after the surgery. And while she was there this chap we're looking for picked her up, persuaded her to go home with him and killed her. And the reason for it—well, I think she must have said something that morning to one of the people she met about meaning to go to talk to Pegler presently about an important matter and been a bit mysterious about it, not wanting to talk openly about your heart attack. But she might have said she knew how serious and dangerous it was, and given this character a completely wrong idea of what she was talking about. So he decided to deal with her before she could do him any damage."

"You keep saying 'he,'" Constance said. "But is it really in your mind that it could have been Naomi? It's she who says she saw Mollie hesitating at the crossroads when Lorna Grace said she set off straight up the lane. I don't know why Naomi should have told a lie about that, but perhaps she did."

Andrew shook his head. "I don't think the nurse saw what Mollie actually did. She drove straight on herself and probably didn't look back at Mollie. But even though a woman could have picked Mollie up and perhaps killed her, I don't think she could have handled her body afterwards. Even if she'd done the murder in the car and then driven straight on to the stream to get rid of her, she'd have had to drag Mollie out of the car into the stream, and I don't think that would have been possible. Anyway, I don't think she was killed in the car. She was stabbed several times and there'd have been a good deal of blood, and there'd certainly have been bloodstains in the car which the police would have found by now. I think she was enticed into somebody's house with the offer of coffee or a drink, and killed perhaps in the kitchen, where it would have been fairly easy to wash the blood away, and then bundled into the car and taken to the stream."

"And about the man in the grey Vauxhall, then?"

The duck arrived and smelled very good, and in attending to it and to the carafe of red wine, it took Andrew a moment to answer Constance's question.

"Ah yes," he said. "As a matter of fact, it's that grey Vauxhall that makes me more suspicious of Naomi than anything else."

"Do you mean you think it was someone she knew?"

"No," Andrew said as he started on his duck, "it's simply that no one but Naomi seems ever to have seen that car, or the man in it, and so I can't help wondering if it really had any existence except in Naomi's imagination, which is known to be fertile. I think possibly she invented the Vauxhall and the man."

"But why?"

"The answer to that might be that she was trying to cover up for someone. If she knew who had killed Mollie and for some reason wanted to protect him, she may have tried to drag a red herring across the path. And she thought of a grey Vauxhall simply because she used to see one in the lane in the days when the Banks family lived in the Gleesons' cottage. She couldn't know that Banks had a perfect alibi for that day, being in police custody."

Constance put down her knife and fork and sat back in her chair.

"I'm sorry," she said, "I can't eat. I thought I could. I thought I wanted to. But I can't."

"Don't worry," Andrew said, though it pained him to think of good roast duckling being wasted. "Have something else. Have some bread and cheese after all."

She shook her head. "No, thank you. But don't let me stop you. I'll just have some wine." She picked up her wineglass and sipped. "So if Naomi's covering up for someone," she went on after a moment, "it looks as if we've got back to Nicholas, doesn't it? Yet he was in Paris when Mike Wakeham disappeared and I can't think of any reason why he should want to kill Colin. So perhaps if they find anything at all when they dig up the dog's grave in the Eckersalls' garden, they're going to find the body of a complete stranger."

"You don't think by any chance Naomi would cover up for Jim Gleeson?"

Constance thought that over before replying and while she did so absentmindedly picked up her knife and fork again and ate a little. Then she ate a little more and seemed to have forgotten that she had thought that she would be unable to eat.

"You know, I can't think of Naomi covering up for the murder of a child," she said. "For a husband or a lover, yes, I can see her doing that. But a child, no. And I don't mean only because I don't think she's got that brand of cruelty and perversity in her. I think it's at least partly because I don't think she'd be sufficiently interested. I think she rather liked Colin, but I don't think she's ever cared much about his disappearance. If she heard he'd been murdered, she'd say, 'Oh dear, that's too bad—I do hope I don't get involved in this.' And certainly she wouldn't take any risks to shield the murderer."

"I see."

Andrew began to think of what was going to happen that afternoon in the Eckersalls' garden. He thought of the decaying body of a Yorkshire terrier being unearthed and then of the digging going on, deep into the subsoil, in the search for another grave, another body.

Thud, thud...

He could imagine the sound of the spades in the hard ground, the growing tension when perhaps the bones of a hand or some rags of clothing were uncovered, and all of a sudden the duck seemed difficult to eat. The sight of Constance quietly proceeding with hers was faintly shocking.

In a hurry to evade that thudding sound in his head, he said, "Of course, you understand why Stonor thanked you for your information about the Gleesons digging up their rose bed."

Constance shook her head. "I can't really say I do."

"It's just that he'd thought of having that done himself. What you told him saved him the trouble. It made him able to concentrate on Timmie's grave, the other place where the ground has been recently disturbed. I believe they're really expecting to find something."

Constance gave her sardonic smile. "Perhaps after all they'll find old Mr. Eckersall there. Has it struck you, Andrew, that that letter that came to Mollie said, 'Don't forget I saw you bury him.' *You*. That can be singular or plural, can't it? So perhaps the letter was meant for the two sisters, who between them could have buried the old man. Of course, the body of a child like Colin could have been handled by one person."

Thud, thud…

Nowadays, Andrew thought, the bare earth of an open grave is tactfully covered at a funeral by a sheet of bright green plastic grass, which is supposed to protect the sensibilities of the grieving from the crude facts of death and decay, though it makes nonsense of the harsh beauty of the burial service. "Earth to earth, dust to dust, ashes to ashes…" Only a few weeks before, he had been at the funeral of an old friend and colleague where, on those words being spoken, the undertaker had delicately taken a polythene bag out of his pocket, had extracted a little earth from it and sprinkled it on the coffin. Andrew had felt that the earth, if it really was earth and not some synthetic substance, had probably been disinfected and deodorized. But if a putrefying corpse were to be dug up in the Eckersalls' garden it would certainly not have been treated with such fastidiousness.

In the end both he and Constance finished their duck and their wine and had some coffee and afterwards walked back to Lindleham, walking very slowly, as if they were both reluctant to arrive and to find out what was being done there. The wind had lessened during the time that they had been in the Swan and patches of blue sky showed here and there amongst the still-hurrying clouds.

On the way they talked very little, but after a while Andrew observed, "You know, Constance, I'm not sure you haven't solved these murders."

"I?" she said incredulously.

"Yes, there are certain things you've said…" He did not finish the sentence, mainly because he was not sure how to finish it. Yet he had another of his hunches concerning what had happened during the past week amongst the people whom he had met here and what would be found when the police dug up the grave of the Yorkshire terrier. He did not want to be there when that occurred and hoped that Constance need not be there either. She had taken enough of an emotional battering already over Mollie's death without requiring any more. If they could reach home and stay there quietly until Superintendent Stonor came to tell them the results of his investigation, it would be best for both of them.

But it was not to be. When they turned at the crossroads into Bell Lane they saw not only that the police were there in force but also that the village of Clareham had somehow become informed that there were events of great interest going forward in Lindleham and had come in considerable numbers to observe, to comment and to share in any excitement that might be generated there. Three police cars were drawn up in a row outside the Eckersalls' gate and several uniformed constables were doing their best to keep the audience at bay, but men, women and children had moved up as close as they were able and were standing in the lane in groups, some tensely silent, some inclined to offer advice to the police or merely demanding to be told what was happening.

When it came to the point, that same curiosity gripped Constance, and she stood still in her gateway, turning to look across the lane towards the Eckersalls' house. She had had some difficulty, apart from penetrating the waiting crowd, in persuading a policeman who wanted to turn her and Andrew back to Clareham that they only wanted to reach her home. Andrew saw that the Gleesons were in their gateway and that Naomi Wakeham was in hers, and on the edge of the crowd farther up the lane he saw Nicholas Ryan.

Jean and Kate Eckersall were in the doorway of their house, their hands tightly clasped together and their eyes fixed with horrified fascination on what was happening in their precious little burial ground under the shadow of the chestnut tree that leant from the Gleesons' garden over theirs. Though the wind had almost died it stirred the branches of the old tree enough to send a shower of petals from the blossom that covered it down over the ground beneath it like confetti being thrown at some fantastic wedding.

But there was very little to be seen. The police had erected canvas screens round the whole dogs' cemetery and no one could tell just what was happening behind them. There was only the sound of spades being thrust over and over again into the ground to tell the watchers that digging was continuing and that nothing had been found yet.

Thud, thud...

Andrew found a quotation taking possession of his mind, but this time for once it was Shakespeare.

Knock, knock! Who's there i' the other devil's name?

Who, if anyone, would they find there when they had dug deep enough? Andrew thought he knew, though he was still not absolutely certain.

A child who was standing in front of him turned round and looked up at him.

"What's happening?" he asked. "What are they doing?"

He was a very dirty child. That was the first thing that Andrew noticed about him. He was far dirtier than any child would be allowed to be in a respectable village like Clareham. Dirt caked his forehead, his cheeks and his neck. It was natural to think that there were probably lice in his hair. He was very thin too, as if it was some time since he had had a good meal. His pullover was filthy and in holes. His jeans were even more stained and tattered than was normal for children of his age, which was about eleven, and long black uncut toenails protruded through what was left of a pair of canvas shoes. His hair was red. The same red as Leslie Gleeson's.

Andrew grasped him by the arm. He had a feeling that if he did not keep tight hold of the child he might vanish away in the crowd in a moment and be lost again.

"You're Colin!" he said.

"Let me go, you're hurting me," the child said.

"Sorry," Andrew said, but he did not loosen his grip. The arm in his grasp was matchstick thin. "Come along, your mother's over there. Can't you see her? Don't you want her?"

The child tried to pull away from him. "No, *he's* there. I don't want to go while *he's* there."

"He won't be there long," Andrew said. "Come along."

"But what's happening?" the boy asked as before. "What are they doing?"

"Never mind about that now. Come on."

Tears began to spill out of the boy's eyes and to make tracks down the dirt on his cheeks.

"Is it because of the dog I killed?" he asked. "I never meant to kill him. Honest. I never thought I could hit him. I never hit anything I aimed at. When he died I was frightened. Is that why they're here—because I killed him?"

"Not exactly," Andrew said. "We'll go into that some other time. Now we'll go and talk to your mother. Don't you want to do that? There's no need to be frightened anymore."

The boy let out a sudden wail and somehow jerked himself free of Andrew's grasp. But it was towards his mother that he ran. She was standing alone in the gateway now. Jim Gleeson had disappeared. A moment before the boy reached her she saw him, gave an incredulous cry of joy and held out her arms to him. He flung himself into them with a look of frenzied hunger and love. Both started crying violently.

There was a sudden stir in the crowd. Andrew had not noticed while he had been talking to Colin that Naomi had left her gate and had returned to her house, but now he saw her car come out of the garage and, driven at reckless speed, swerve out through the gate, shoot through the crowd, which scattered to right and left in panic, and disappear down the lane towards Clareham. He had a glimpse of Naomi's face before she vanished, white and set and crazed with fear. At the same moment he realized that the thudding of the spades had stopped. There was silence in the Eckersalls' garden.

Andrew and Constance waited side by side until Stonor appeared from behind the canvas screens, then Andrew went towards him.

"You've found him?" he said.

"Yes."

"Wakeham?"

"Yes."

"Murdered by his wife, I believe," Andrew said, "who murdered Mollie Baird and David Pegler also. She's just taken off for Clareham in a hurry, but no doubt you'll be able to pick her up quite soon, unless she crashes her car first, which I think she might. I don't think she knows what she's doing. But you can still get Gleeson, her accomplice, if you hurry. It'll save you the trouble of chasing him."

Andrew was right about Naomi's fate. At the crossroads she did not turn left into Clareham, but drove straight on along the narrow winding lane beyond. Whether or not she had any clear idea of where she was going no one was ever to know, for at a bend in the lane she drove at seventy head-on into a lorry. The crash did not kill her, but she was dead by the time she arrived at the hospital in Maddingleigh. The driver of the lorry also had to be taken to the hospital and treated for shock.

Meanwhile it was announced on radio and television that evening that a man was helping the police with their inquiries into the murders of Michael Wakeham, Mollie Baird and David Pegler. Later Jim Gleeson was charged with being an accessory to the three murders and was remanded in custody.

Andrew remained in Lindleham until after the inquest into Mollie's death and her funeral. Before that he had heard that small smears of blood that matched hers had been found on the floor of Naomi's kitchen, although this had been energetically scrubbed, and there were more in the boot of Jim Gleeson's car. But before that, in the evening after the body of Mike Wakeham had been disinterred, Andrew and Constance had had some time to themselves. She had been very quiet and, as Andrew had been able to see, had been turning something over in her mind, trying to work out its meaning before consulting him.

At last she said, "When we were on our way home from the Swan, Andrew, you said you thought I might have solved these murders. Why did you say that?"

"There were two things you said," he answered. "You said you couldn't imagine Naomi covering up for the murder of a child, that she just wouldn't be interested. At the time we thought it was possible that Gleeson might have murdered Colin, though Wakeham was also a possible victim. And if it was Wakeham, who was the likeliest person to have killed him? Naomi herself, of course. In cases like this, the husband or wife is always the first suspect. And whom would she really try to cover up for with her story of the imaginary Vauxhall? Who but herself? Who else did she ever care about? But if she killed Wakeham, which for all we'll ever know she may have done defending herself when he attacked her in a fit of jealous rage when he somehow found out she'd a lover, she couldn't have buried him. If she killed him in their house, she couldn't possibly have disposed of the body. A body's a heavy, unwieldy thing to handle. So it meant that she'd an accomplice. And who was the most probable one? You thought of Nicholas as a possible murderer. But he'd an alibi for the time Wakeham disappeared, so I began to think of Gleeson. His wife was often out in the evenings, you'd told me, at meetings of the Women's Institute or pottery classes, and it would have been easy for him and Naomi to meet in the Gleesons' cottage. She'd have concocted one of her remarkable stories to explain to her husband why she had to go out. Perhaps she said she was taking lessons in Russian in Maddingleigh, or something equally colourful. But he didn't quite believe her and discovered what was happening and there was a quarrel which left him dead, killed with a kitchen knife, and her with a corpse on her hands. So what did she do? She telephoned her lover, of course, and between them they took Wakeham's body to the Eckersalls' garden and buried him in the freshly dug patch of earth where the sisters had buried their dog before taking off for the Highlands. A pretty laborious job even though the ground had been dug over recently, and

Gleeson, who of course did the digging, hurt his back and has been having trouble with it ever since. And Pegler, driving home down the lane from a late call, saw them doing it and started the dangerous game of blackmail."

"You said there were two things that helped to solve the murder," Constance said. "What was the other thing?"

"Only that the word *you* can be singular or plural," Andrew answered. "Until then I hadn't thought seriously of Naomi as being involved in the murders. I thought it might be Gleeson who had killed either Colin or Wakeham and been seen by Pegler, but the obvious thing hadn't occurred to me that he could have seen two people doing the job and was putting the screw on them both."

"And you think it was Naomi who killed both Mollie and David?"

"That's how it looks to me. She told us she overtook Mollie at the crossroads and offered her a lift home and Mollie refused it. I think Naomi must have told us about having seen Mollie there because she knew someone had seen them talking and might remember it. She may have thought Nurse Grace could have seen them before she drove off. But I don't think Mollie did refuse the lift. I think Naomi had some sob story about the husband who had abandoned her and how badly she needed to talk to someone, and poor, kind Mollie went with her and was taken into the kitchen to help make some coffee and was stabbed to death there. And then, of course, Naomi had another corpse on her hands, so she rang up Gleeson, who she knew hadn't gone to work that day because he was going to see the doctor, and again he disposed of the body. But this time it had to be done in a hurry, before Leslie got home from the sale in Maddingleigh, and who might want the car later in the day and anyway who'd want to know why he had to go out in the evening if he waited for darkness. So he bundled Mollie into the car and dumped her in the stream, taking the appalling risk of being seen. But he got away with it for the time being. And then, of course, they had to dispose of Pegler."

"You think Mollie told Naomi that morning, when they met in the shop before Mollie went to the surgery, that she'd something important to discuss with David and Naomi misunderstood what it was."

"Yes, because you've got to remember that either Naomi or Gleeson had had a letter from Pegler thanking whichever of them it was for a contribution to the building of the new cricket pavilion, when neither of them had made any contribution. I think the person who probably did was Nicholas. And Naomi, who was getting used to murder, or possibly had even begun to enjoy it, and who'd no wife who'd want to know why her husband suddenly had to go out in the evening, went down to Pegler's house and repeated the stabbing business, in which she must have become quite proficient, and slipped quietly home. There was no need to get rid of the body that time. It wasn't in her house. She could leave him where he fell, to be discovered in the morning."

Constance nodded thoughtfully, accepting Andrew's reconstruction of the events of the last few days.

"How long ago did you think of all this?" she asked.

"Well, I told you I had a hunch about it, didn't I?" he said. "But I couldn't be sure of it till I knew who the victim was. So I suppose you can say I didn't really know what to think till that child Colin spoke to me."

It was that same evening that Leslie and Colin visited Constance.

Colin by then had been put into a bath and been scrubbed from head to foot, as well as presentably reclothed. It seemed probable to Andrew that he had also been fed, yet when Constance produced a plateful of potato crisps to go with the milk that she offered him while the adults settled for whisky, he snatched up a handful of them and stuffed them into his mouth, chewing them up and swallowing them down as if he were afraid they might vanish if he did not dispose of them quickly. Apart from that he was subdued and disinclined to talk. Leslie apologized for his behaviour.

"You know, he's really frightened of not having enough to eat," she said. "I don't know how long it's going to take to fill the great yawning emptiness of his stomach. D'you know how he's been living all this last month? I hardly like to tell you. He's been stealing. Begging too sometimes, going into shops and looking pathetic and being given a meat pie or something. But mostly he's been shoplifting from supermarkets, and stealing from stalls in street markets and people's gardens and sometimes even from hen houses, taking the eggs and eating them raw. And he's been sleeping in churches. He'd creep in before they shut them up for the night and hide somewhere, then make himself a bed of the hassocks and really be quite comfortable and slip out in the morning before the early service. Of course, he never washed. Then he came across a group of young people who were living in a ruined cottage he doesn't seem to know quite where, and they took him in and looked after him as well as they could, though they didn't seem to have much money themselves, or anything to eat but tins of beans. And when they asked who he was and where he came from, he said he couldn't remember. Quite clever of him, really."

There was an odd note of pride in Leslie's voice, as if she felt that there was something admirable in her son's capacity for survival.

She went on: "But then one of them saw a television programme when he was passing a shop that sold radios and things, and it happened there was a picture of Colin on the screen just then, with an appeal to anyone who saw him to contact the police. Well, they didn't do that, because they weren't the sort of people who'd ever go to the police about anything, but they told Colin how terrible his mother must be feeling, and they gave him some money and put him on a train to Maddingleigh, then he took a bus to get here. And I wish I could thank them, but he doesn't know anything about them except that they were called Barry and Terry and Tracey and Sue. When he first came home he wouldn't say anything about what he'd been doing. He only cried and cried and ate and ate.

But then suddenly he started talking and it's been going on ever since. I expect there's lots more to come. Oh, Constance, you don't know how I feel, having him safe at home again when I was sure he'd died some horrible death. It's just as if I'd come out of some terrible black cloud into daylight."

"And Jim?" Constance asked.

Leslie said nothing for a moment, then with the excitement quenched in her voice, answered quietly, "Let's not talk about that. I haven't begun to take it in yet. Awful as it is, it's a kind of relief to know I'm going to be free again. I loved him once, but it seems a long time ago. Some day perhaps I'll be able to forget it all. I know it's desperately selfish, but all that really matters to me now is that I've got Colin back."

The plate of potato crisps was empty. Colin looked hungrily up at Constance, who got up obligingly and went to get some more.

When at last Andrew was able to return to London, he and Constance took an affectionate farewell of one another and agreed that they would meet for lunch as soon as this was convenient for Constance. She drove him to the station in Maddingleigh and left him there to buy his ticket and a copy of the *Financial Times*, which was his favourite reading on short train journeys.

Making his way on to the platform where the London train was expected, he sat down on a bench to wait. He was at least twenty minutes earlier than he need have been, but he had a habit of arriving considerably earlier than was necessary to catch trains and planes. He could not remember that he had ever missed one by being late, but there was always an anxiety at the back of his mind that one day it would happen. Since he was as fond of Constance as he was, he was a little disturbed to discover how peaceful it felt to be sitting there on the platform with only strangers around him who had no interest in him whatever.

Then his feeling of peace was shattered by someone sitting down beside him and saying, "Hallo."

It was Nicholas Ryan. He had a suitcase with him, which made it look as if he were not going to London merely for the day.

"Hallo," Andrew said. "Going home?"

"Yes, thank God," Nicholas said. "I've sold the house, you know. Anyway, subject to contract. But I think the sale will go through all right. The people really seem to want it. It's going to be a home for handicapped children. I'd as soon that as anything. And I've got a good price for it, considering how singularly unattractive it is."

Andrew felt curious what the price had been, but since Nicholas did not volunteer to tell him this, was too well-mannered to ask.

"I expect you're glad to be getting home to London too," Nicholas went on. "No trouble but having your television stolen occasionally when you're out, and being mugged from time to time, and now and then hearing an I.R.A. bomb go off somewhere nearby. Peace itself. I hope I never have to go back to Lindleham."

Andrew answered with a grunt. He was glad to see his train coming in, and although he and Nicholas climbed companionably into the same carriage and sat down side by side, it turned out that Nicholas had a copy of *The Guardian* with him and Andrew was free to read the *Financial Times*. He did his best on the way to Paddington to discover whether his modest investments had been going up or down recently, and although he was never sure that he understood such matters, he was inclined to think that perhaps they had gone up a little. This was always cheering, even though he almost never did any buying or selling of stocks, so slight fluctuations in their value really made no difference to his financial position.

At Paddington he took a taxi to his flat and arrived there, kicked off his shoes, leaving them lying in the middle of the sitting-room floor, padded out comfortably in his socks to the kitchen, made sure that the woman who came in twice a week to clean his flat had followed the instructions that he had sent to her on a postcard, asking her to buy bread, butter and ham for him so that he could make himself some sandwiches for lunch, then poured out a whisky and settled down with it in the sitting room to enjoy the silent company of Robert Hooke.

Andrew had had some interesting ideas about him while he had been away. They involved tearing up most of what he had already written and beginning again at the beginning. But what of it?

Suddenly he realized that he was talking aloud to himself, which was something that he had not done all the time that he had been in Lindleham.

> *Never, I ween, did swimmer,*
> *In such an evil case,*
> *Struggle through such a raging flood,*
> *Safe to the landing place...*

It was most annoying, most unnecessary to have Horatius still pursuing him. Why could he not have left him behind at Cherry Tree Cottage? And to describe what he had been through there as a raging flood was certainly an exaggeration. All the same, it was pleasant, very pleasant, to have reached such a safe landing place as his quiet flat.

We hope you loved *The Other Devil's Name*.

We love it, too, and in fact, we are altogether hooked on gently witty tales of amateur sleuthery. With that in mind, we thought you might enjoy *Hidden Agenda*, by Anna Porter. First in the Judith Hayes series, *Agenda* is set in Toronto (for an English-but-not-really flavor), and it stars one of our all-time favorite journalist-detectives, poking her nose into what turns out to be an unexpectedly sophisticated series of odd events.

We've attached the first few chapters. If you'd like to read further, *Hidden Agenda* is available wherever fine books are sold. You can also visit our website for a tasty selection of sample chapters from even more titles—try before you buy, at felonyandmayhem.com/collections/book-excerpts!

Hidden Agenda

One

No one likes to think about suicides. Least of all, the men who run the subways.

On the night of April 8, 1985, at 11:05 p.m., as his train was rounding the bend in the tunnel just before Summerhill, it was the last thing motorman John Hogg wished to think about. On the downtown run Summerhill and Rosedale are the last of the suburban stations and on a weeknight almost no one gets on. The yellow lights make the platforms seem unreal. He could slow the train, slide into a fast stop, open and close the doors in almost the same movement, and start again as fast, for sport. Something to keep his mind off that other time. As he pulled out of Summerhill, Hogg began to unwrap his chicken sandwich.

When approaching the next stop, Rosedale, late at night, Hogg always had that same nightmare feeling, fear gripping his jaws tight and catching in his throat. His first suicide had been at Rosedale Station. In the heart of chic, residential old-world Toronto, where he sometimes took the kids for a Sunday drive to show them the palatial, Georgian homes.

Then, also, it had been late at night. The girl in front of the train no more than a blur of movement...

He had to stop thinking about it.

Most drivers didn't like the late shift, it cut into their family lives, but Hogg had asked for it. And got it. There were a few privileges to be had for twenty-three years on the trains. The kids were grown now, the wife was taking some damn-fool course at Ryerson, and he could get the day to himself. Peaceful. And some nights there were parties. Tonight should be a great one. One of his pals was retiring from the "service" (that's what they called it, like the army), and they were all getting together. No wives. Just the boys. And he'd heard a rumor someone had lined up a couple of strippers—for laughs.

He was running a few minutes behind schedule, the lights were green all the way, so he moved the speed lever to 75 and took another bite of the sandwich. A little dry. He was coming in fast, past that infernal cut-off where the platform starts...

He felt it before he saw it. A heavy thump-crunch. A shudder as it smashed into the front. Train slowed by the impact. A shoe hit the window at eye level. Brown. Brown spray splattered the glass. He ducked involuntarily before starting to apply the air-brakes. Somebody screamed. Oh god, no, it can't be. *Not here.*

"For chrissakes, John, stop the fucking car," he heard the guard yell into the microphone.

It was only then that he slammed on the emergency brakes, and pulled the train up, wheels shrieking, halfway down the platform. He jerked open his door.

There were three passengers in the front car. A young man, scrambling from the floor. A young woman, white-faced, holding onto the vertical bar with both hands. She looked at him, eyes wide, her mouth sagging open. Another woman was screaming, hiccuping for breath, her head thrown back. Hogg muttered something at the young woman. *Regulation: calm the passengers so as to prevent panic. They must stay inside the car until the police arrive.*

He reached back into his cubicle and pressed the alarm button, then walked to the first door, withdrew the emergency pass key from his breast pocket and opened it.

"Please, everybody, stay calm. Stay seated. The police will be here in a few minutes," he said to the man who was moving toward him.

He ran to the emergency alarm station at the end of the platform, broke the glass protection strip, pressed the trip lever down to cut rail power. Then he picked up the red phone, and dialed Transit Control. *Dial 555 for suicides.*

"It's a 555 at Rosedale. This is 2454—Hogg," he added unnecessarily. They would know anyway, as soon as he dialed, where he was and what had happened. They would also notify Police Communications who would direct police officers, ambulance and CIB personnel to the scene.

When Hogg turned, Jake Moore, the guard, was already at the front, bending to look under the train. Hogg jumped down to join him.

"Jeesus, what a lot of blood," he said. One of the two front fenders was bent and twisted out of shape. "That's where he must have hit." Blood splattered all over both fenders, and the lower half of the window. "There he is." Jake was on his hands and knees, pointing down under the belly of the car. There was an arm sticking out over the inside rail. An arm in a raincoat-sleeve, wrist wearing a gold watchstrap. "He's got to be dead," Jake said.

Hogg didn't say anything, he just nodded. No one could have survived that.

"Didn't you have another one here a couple of years back?" Jake asked.

"Yeah. A girl... She was just gone fifteen."

"What foul luck. Twice in the same place." Jake crouched down again to get a better look under the train.

"Did you see him jump?" he asked.

"No. I mean, yes, I must have. It all happened so fast."

"I thought you'd never stop the car," Jake said quietly.

Hogg became aware of other people on the platform, a small cluster with their feet at Hogg's shoulder level. Silent. Staring.

"Would all passengers please clear the platform," said the loudspeaker.

"Shit. I had to slow down first, didn't I? People get hurt if you stop too suddenly," Hogg blurted out, angry. "Your first one this, isn't it?"

Jake nodded.

"You'll learn."

They climbed back onto the platform.

"There's been an accident. Everybody please go upstairs," Hogg said.

"Everybody please clear the platform," the loudspeaker tuned in.

The spectators backed away, slowly. They made no move toward the stairs.

"Did you see what happened?" one of them asked.

"I saw him when he came down. Such a nice-looking man."

"Do you suppose he jumped?"

Hogg checked his watch. They were, as ever, efficient, he thought with some pride. The line supervisor was coming along the platform, waving people upstairs. Sensing the authority of the gesture, they began to move. It was 11:18.

Behind the supervisor's gray uniform, Hogg could see four other men in brown—Equipment Department and Track Patrol.

"You're Hogg?" the supervisor asked. "Where did it happen?"

"As I was entering the station. He came at me from the side. There was no way...hell, I couldn't even see him."

The supervisor scanned the side of the train for pieces of clothing, or body. Two of the other men were down on the tracks looking under the train. None of them were first-timers on the "jumper squad."

"Under car one. About in line with door one," a Track Patrol man shouted at the approaching police officers.

"Ambulance here yet?"

"On the way."

One of the policemen pulled out the emergency wooden box from the south end of the platform, broke the seal and pulled out the basket stretcher, a rubber sheet, and the chalk for marking the location of the body.

The doctor and two St. John's Ambulance men in white uniforms crawled under the train to determine whether the man was dead. Not that there was any real doubt. Still, one has to follow regulations; it's what makes the job bearable.

"He's dead all right," the doctor said, emerging from under the car. He wiped his hands on his white coat, leaving black and brown smears alongside the pockets. His face was flushed and damp as a policeman helped him up onto the platform.

"OK, everybody off the track. We'll have to move the train to get it out," said the officer in charge. "You the motorman?" he asked Hogg.

Hogg nodded.

In five more minutes they had the body on the stretcher. Most of the body. One arm arrived separately. It had been thrown across the meridian divide toward the Northbound lane.

The back of the head had been smashed. Some soft gray jelly lay beside the face. Blood caked over the forehead, across the neck and down the length of his fur-lined trench coat. The first impact must have broken bones in every part of the man's body, though all you could see was where his chest had caved in. He was covered in dirt, mud and black tar from the undercarriage. Still, he had been a handsome man. Maybe mid-fifties, hair brown to beginning white, face lined by too many smiles, gray-blue eyes staring up at the doctor's hand as he closed the lids, firmly.

Sergeant Levine was jotting in his notebook, policeman's shorthand, while he waited for the CIB photographer. Hogg let him into the first car so he could talk to the passengers. None of them had seen anything, so Levine let them go. The two women were going to take cabs home.

Levine returned to take stock of the man's personal belongings. The doctor, because regulations said he was the one to do it, had removed the blood-soaked wallet and some credit cards from the breast pocket and a cluster of keys, a pair of kid-leather gloves, gold-rimmed reflector-lens sunglasses, some business cards and a checkbook from the other pockets.

As soon as Levine saw that his partner had finished outlining the position of the body, he turned to Hogg who was waiting beside him.

"How did it happen?" he asked, pencil at the ready, not looking up from his notebook.

"I was coming into the station when he jumped. Must have been standing right by the wall. Couldn't really see much. Just a blur. Then his shoe hit the window."

"How fast were you traveling?"

"About 65 and slowing for the station," said Hogg, a little uncertainly, but who would know anyway?

Levine looked up at the line supervisor: "May as well get your show back on the road. I'll talk to the other witnesses upstairs."

"You'd better let Jake Moore take over at the controls," the supervisor said to Hogg.

"We'll have a relief crew waiting at Bloor. You guys take what's left of the night off." Then he jogged to the end of the platform to call Transit Control and ask them to restore traction power.

The two men with the stretcher were already climbing the stairs.

Hogg went into the guard's cubicle. Nobody asked any questions. At 11:31 the train was on its way again. Twenty-one to twenty-two minutes, Hogg thought: they've got it down to a fine art.

Detective Inspector David Parr arrived as the stretcher was leaving. As the officer in charge at Jarvis Street Station on Monday nights he should have been there earlier, but he was in the middle of questioning a particularly hostile assault and battery witness, and gaining momentum, when the call came. The case was coming up for trial within the week, so Parr had decided it wouldn't matter if he was a little late. Not a hell of a lot you can do for a suicide anyway.

Moving past the stretcher, he flicked the white sheet aside, looked briefly into the dead man's face, and continued on with a nod to the ambulance men.

"Bloody mess, eh?" he said to the constable who was bringing up the rear. "You'll notify the coroner?"

"Yes, sir," the constable said. "Sergeant Levine was taking inventory."

Parr waved him on and went to stand beside Levine at the edge of the platform.

"All over?" he asked cheerfully.

"It is now," Levine said, as one of the men in brown overalls scrambled up over the lip of the platform and handed him a highly polished tan leather shoe. Levine turned it over; it had hardly been worn. "Good as new," he said. "Look at that." He pointed to the gold printed label inside the shoe. "A Gucci, yet. Why anyone with a pair of brand-new Guccis would want to throw himself at a moving train, I'll never know."

The supervisor came over to tell them he was letting people through at the top again. The two policemen fell in line behind him as he started up the stairs.

"Who was he?" Parr asked.

Levine shrugged. He handed over the plastic bag with the contents of the pockets, holding it between thumb and forefinger as if it were some nasty insect.

"Here," he said. "You can have the shoe too. Pick up its mate over at the morgue. He won't need them. Not where he's going."

"Perks go with the job, eh?" Parr smiled as he rummaged through the contents. "Here we are." He pulled a driver's license out of the wallet. "George Harris, sixty years old. Lived at 24 Rose Hill Drive. That's not far from here."

"You'll be going over there tonight?" Levine asked.

"Yes. Soon as this is over."

"Don't you ever do it by phone?"

"Not if I can help it," Parr said quietly. "I sure as hell wouldn't like to be told on the phone. Would you?"

The supervisor interrupted them, opening the door to a small staff room near the Yonge Street exit.

"There were only six people on the platform," he said. "They're all in here."

"Good evening." Parr smiled encouragement as he entered. "We won't want to keep you long. Just a few questions and you can all be on your way again."

Six faces glared at him, silent. In shock, Parr thought. Suicides are damned unsettling.

In the corner, a kid about twenty with short-cropped, greased brown hair, leather jacket, tight blue jeans, scuffed leather boots, not quite punk but thinking about it. He held hands with a girl, same age, long damp hair, pale pinched skin. She huddled close to him, touching his body with hers. She seemed docile and needy. He was defiant. At his age, that was fashionable.

By the window there was a black woman, late fifties, soft felt hat pulled down low over her nose, worn khaki raincoat too narrow and too short, orange Dacron dress. She was holding a white supermarket shopping bag, her arms wrapped around it. She looked scared. Might have weathered some bad times with the law; more likely, she was an illegal.

A man, about thirty-five, sat uncomfortably straight-backed at the narrow table, an ashtray in front of him, his briefcase tucked between his navy-blue lace-ups. He wore a three-piece negotiating-blue suit, tinted rimless glasses, and was smoking his third cigarette. He had an exceptionally thin long neck with a jumpy Adam's apple tucked into his tight white collar.

The other end of the table was occupied by a man in his forties—balding, red-faced—and a pinched, matronly woman, possibly English. Clearly they were not together. They were a study in contrasts. She had half-turned away from him, balancing her outsize monogrammed handbag against the table leg. She wore a black mink coat, casually unbuttoned, her elegant knees composed over each other, foot tapping in anticipation. The man was sweating. He took a crumpled Kleenex from his lumberjack shirt pocket, shook it out, and wiped his forehead.

Levine flicked open his notebook.

"Could we please have your names and addresses? Police procedure, I'm afraid," he said deferentially. "Perhaps you'd like to get the ball rolling." He turned to the executive type, who was closest.

"Joseph Muller, 27 Roseborough," he said, shaking another cigarette out of the package. "Do we get called for an inquest or something?"

"I don't think that will be necessary," Parr said. "Phone number?"

Levine wrote down both the home and business numbers. A stockbroker going home late. Edgy.

"When did you arrive on the platform?" Parr asked.

"Couple of minutes before the train. I wasn't even near him when he jumped..."

"Did you see him jump?" Parr asked quickly.

"Well... I sort of saw a movement, out of the corner of my eye really. Then there was this awful thud."

"Was he already on the platform when you came down?"

"I don't know, really. I don't remember. I was reading the paper." He waved his rolled-up *Star* at Parr.

Parr thanked him and opened the door to let him out before turning to the others.

The apprentice punk hadn't seen anything. Nor had the girl. It was the thud she remembered. Her lower lip trembled when she spoke. While Parr questioned them the boy was pumping her hand, his eyes steady with hostility.

"Get them out of here," Parr murmured to Levine.

The man in the lumberjack shirt said he was a cab driver named Jenkins, taking a day off. "Teach me to take the gawddamned train," he grumbled. He had seen Harris march to the edge of the platform, lean out to look up the track when they heard the train coming, then back up as if to get out of the way. But he didn't. He had sort of lurched forward again and fallen in front of it. Somebody screamed.

"Who?" Parr asked, but none of the remaining passengers admitted to screaming, so he went on with the questions.

The black woman, not unexpectedly, had heard nothing and seen nothing. She was so eager to get away Parr could feel her vibrating toward the door. He hoped they wouldn't have to call her or that she had given a false address. He wasn't going to harass her for identification. Rotten luck for her to be in the wrong place at the wrong time.

They had left the gray-haired woman to last. She seemed content sipping her tea, listening with grave interest, like a schoolteacher watching the class take turns at reading. That is what she turned out to be: Mrs. W.A. Hall, a retired schoolteacher. The husband must have made the money.

She had seen Harris coming onto the platform. His right hand had been in his trouser pocket. His raincoat was open, loose, the belt swinging as he walked. Such a distinguished-looking man, graying at the temples. Couldn't have been much more than fifty. He had hurried to the end of the platform—the north end.

"To think now what his purpose was!" she said with a sigh. "What a horrible waste. And why would anyone choose such a messy way?"

"Did you actually see him jump?"

"No. I heard him hit, though. Sounded like a ripe pumpkin hitting the pavement. It was the black woman who screamed. She kept screaming afterward too. Very emotional they are, on the islands. Though I daresay they see more violent deaths than we do. She wasn't so far from where I was. I saw she had her mouth open. She'd dropped her bag." She was quite certain the black woman must have seen the man jump.

Parr offered to drive Mrs. Hall home. It was more or less on his way.

She obviously enjoyed the idea of sitting in a police car. Her one regret was that Detective Inspector Parr would not tell her the name of the deceased. He couldn't, before notifying the next-of-kin.

Chapter Two

Judith decided it was time for her to draw up a will. Nothing fancy, mind you, no heavy legalese, just the basics, in her own words. At age thirty-eight, a responsible person must have a will. Even if she wasn't consistently responsible. A will is something like a stocktaking.

> *I, Judith Hayes, being of sound mind* (mostly) *and body* (still holding on), *do on this day, April 9, 1985, leave all my clothes to my daughter Anne. My new slingback sandals can be held in trust for her until she is old enough to wear them. She's certainly big enough to wear them. My son, Jimmy, can have the typewriter, and the two of them can wrangle over the couch, the chairs and all the stuff in the kitchen. They can have their own beds. They can split the insurance dough. Their father had better take over the mortgage payments on the house. For all I care, he can even move in with them. I don't wish to have my kids move to Chicago and live with him.*

She wondered if she could be quite as specific in a will and whether her instructions would be followed because they were in a will. Could James just declare himself legal guardian, or next-of-kin, or whatever, sell off the house (all the blood-sweat-and-tears to keep it these past seven years) and move the kids to that glass and chrome tower he called home in Chicago? She should probably postpone all thoughts of dying until she had ascertained what her rights would be afterward.

She climbed out of bed and padded down to the kitchen to make herself a cup of coffee. Naturally there was no milk in the fridge. Anne drank about a quart a day, and all those brilliant plans for the kids to keep an up-to-date shopping list on the little blackboard Judith had bought for the purpose had long been abandoned. The idea had been that when you finished something, you wrote it on the board.

No bread either. She didn't care so much about that, but the kids would notice when they got out the jar of peanut butter for their early morning treat. Serve them right.

The black coffee tasted stale, but it would wake her up and might get rid of the pounding in her head. There was a time when she could stay up till 4:00 a.m. drinking, talking and smoking cigarettes. Now, just a few drinks and she had a thumping hangover. Still, she was entitled to one the day after her thirty-eighth birthday. Fair way on the downhill slope. What gets you is knowing all the things you will never be when you grow up. For example, she would never be a great dramatic actress, or a ballet star, or a famous inventor. She'd never even be rich, damn it. Not even the editor of the lousy *Toronto Star*, let alone *The New Yorker*. Self-pity, Marsha had said…on your thirty-eighth birthday you are entitled to indulge in some self-pity. And double martinis on the rocks—hang your diet—and chain-smoking that last package of Rothmans Specials, and staying up until you're ready to drop—alone, or otherwise. She had had a few friends over for a late dinner, but had never quite found the courage to tell them what the occasion was. Allan Goodman had come with two bottles of Asti Spumante, a poor substitute for champagne, and barely enough to go around, but OK for toasting an evening if you weren't having a birthday. And it hadn't been Allan's fault;

he didn't know. After they left, she had brought out the cake with all thirty-eight pink candles, all her wishes ready before she blew them out. Then she had finished the entire pitcher of martinis. She vaguely remembered having had a discreet little cry on the expedition up the stairs to her bedroom.

After a thorough search, she located the Alka Seltzer and managed to drink about half a glassful without gagging. The rest of it had stopped fizzing anyway. She took her coffee mug upstairs. In turn, as she passed, she banged on the kids' doors and opened them slightly.

"Time for another fun day at school."

She had got the idea of banging before she opened the door about a year ago when she found Jimmy examining his balls in the mirror. He had been furious at the intrusion. And she had been a little startled herself.

Anne was pulling her jeans on already. Amazing how that kid never had any trouble waking up.

"Hey, Mum," she said over one bony shoulder, "had quite a night last night, didn't you? How is the happy birthday girl this morning?"

"Don't ask," said Judith plaintively. "I doubt if I shall survive the day, let alone the next year."

"Why don't you go back to bed? We'll make our own breakfast."

"Can you get Jimmy out of the sack for me?"

As Judith crawled in between the cooling sheets she heard Anne's familiar hollering at her brother and the equally familiar grumbling reply. Then the phone rang.

"May I speak to Mrs. Hayes?" a polite male voice enquired.

"I think so," said Judith cautiously. "Who shall I say is calling?"

"Detective Inspector Parr, of the Toronto Police Department." A pause. *My god, they're on to me. Parking tickets... those parking tickets I haven't paid. They're going to put me in jail.* She was still trying to clear her throat when the polite voice came back on the line.

"Hello. Is this Judith Hayes speaking?"

"Yes. This is she," Judith said firmly and grammatically, remembering to show no weakness in front of the police or they'll suspect you of more than you've committed. An armed robber she had once interviewed in the Kingston pen had given her that piece of advice. Why was it that policemen always made her feel guilty, even now that most of them were younger than she was?

"Mrs. Hayes, I'm afraid I have rather bad news for you," said Parr, in the soft, modulated tone he had developed for such occasions. "Mr. George Harris died late last night. It was a... sudden...death." He let that sink in, then went on quickly, "I was told by Mrs. Harris that you were with her husband yesterday. I wondered if I might come around and ask you a few questions."

Oh god.

Parr waited a while, then asked: "You did see him yesterday?"

"How did he...?" Judith choked on the last word. She was going to call him today. He had looked so well. Happy, really.

"It happened on the subway," Parr said not very helpfully. "You *did* see him yesterday?"

"Yes, we spent a couple of hours together. Did he have a heart attack? Did you say on the subway?"

"We haven't determined the cause of death yet," Parr interrupted. "May I come over this morning? It will only take a few minutes."

"Well, I had planned to..." Oh, what the hell. The day lay about her in ruins already. "Why?"

"It would appear you may have been the last person to talk to Mr. Harris. Routine questions, Mrs. Hayes. It's what we do."

"OK," she said, hesitating.

"Fine. I'll be there in ten minutes."

"Now, wait a minute. I've only just..." but the line was already dead. Damn him. Inconsiderate bastard.

She jumped out of bed, yanked her nightgown over her head, threw it back onto the pillow in almost the same movement and grabbed some underwear from the top drawer of her dresser.

"There's no bread," Jimmy said accusingly. He was leaning against the open door wearing torn jeans, a stretched sweater and his best tough-male pose. Cute.

"I have no time for that now, Jimmy. If you want bread, you can write it on the blackboard, or you can get it yourself." She took out a bulky black sweater. Like Jimmy's, it was guaranteed to hide all imperfections. Color appropriate too. What the hell did George have to go and die for anyway?

"Something wrong, Mum?" Jimmy's voice rose a little and he abandoned the hunched-shoulders-forward segment of the macho stance.

"Somebody I know just died." No tears. Swallow hard.

"Who?"

"George Harris, the publisher. You met him. He was a friend." She pulled on a pair of tailored slacks. They were new, with razor-sharp seams, and made her feel a little less like falling over.

"Hey, Anne," Jimmy yelled. "Can you put the kettle on? Mum would like another cup of coffee."

If Judith had had time, she would have gone over and hugged him. As it was, she just smiled at him in the mirror.

"You should see yourself," Jimmy said helpfully. "Must have had quite a night of it."

"You should see *yourself*," growled Judith. "I still remember when you liked to have your pants in one piece. Takes some asshole in the East End of London to start it, and all you kids think it's cool to have more holes than pants. Cool all right. Specially in the middle of April." Jimmy shuffled his feet for a second. Then he must have decided to let it go. She loved him for it.

Judith examined her face in the bathroom mirror. Even in this dim light it looked dreadful. Dark patches under the eyes, slight sag where the lines were etching themselves further in. She breathed in deeply to make sure her lungs were both still there, then alternated splashing hot water and cold water on her face.

"Jimmy just told me about Mr. Harris dying," Anne said as she deposited a cup of coffee on the cracked toilet lid. "Terrible. He was such a nice man." Anne sat on the rim of the bathtub.

"He wasn't that old, was he?" Jimmy asked.

"Look you two, I'd love to have your company for the rest of the day, but you have school and I have a policeman coming around in about five minutes. So please…"

They left, reluctantly.

"Are you going to be all right?" Anne asked from the stairs.

"Yes. I'll be fine, thank you. I mean I'll be OK." Judith coated her face with darker-than-skintone, cover-all, pan-stick makeup. It smoothed over the creases and added a touch of color.

"Not much of a birthday, is it?" Anne yelled.

"Your presents were good. Jimmy, where did you find that chime?"

"Chinatown. I wanted silk slippers but didn't know your size."

"Marsha's coming today, isn't she?"

"I sure hope so."

Judith outlined her eyelids in gray. It was a good color to lift up the green of her eyes, which needed all the help they could get. She picked a smoke-black mascara and pale lipstick.

"Are you kids still down there?" she shouted, feeling a little stronger. She never knew what to say or how to behave, other than busy, when people died—she had never been a good weeper. Must be a fear of losing control—that was Marsha's theory, at any rate. Marsha had endless theories about human behavior, and she had majored in Judith's special fears.

"Mum, I'll get the bread," Jimmy called, "and milk. OK? You can pay me back later."

Fabulous kids.

"Great. Thanks. Listen, tell you what, I'll make you guys a sumptuous dinner if you come home in time. We can all eat together."

Detective Inspector Parr was at the door. Judith grabbed for her hairbrush and whipped it through her long auburn hair. It needed washing, but even so, it was her best feature.

Anne opened the door and she and Jimmy left, making room for Parr to enter.

Detective Parr was not the type. The last time she had talked to a police detective, he had been ex-army, sturdy and square-shouldered. This one was thin and angular, fortyish, tall enough to have to duck at the door. His eyes squinted under heavy eyebrows. He wore a tweed jacket with oversize brown buttons, dark-gray pants, a creased white shirt open at the neck and a stained blue-gray tie that had slipped askew.

"Mrs. Hayes?"

"Yes. Detective Inspector Parr, I assume. Come on in," Judith said coolly since he was already progressing toward the living room. He threw his raincoat over the back of a chair and scanned the room quickly. "Must have had a bit of a party here last night," he smiled.

"A birthday party. Sort of. Do sit down."

He chose a straight-backed chair by the dining room table and pushed aside a few of last night's dishes, all business.

"We'll make it as brief as possible." He flicked open his notebook. "I understand you were interviewing Mr. Harris yesterday."

"Yes, I was commissioned by *Saturday Night* magazine to write a profile of George Harris and his publishing house. Yesterday was our second interview."

"You've known him for some time?" Parr said.

"Yes. I worked for him once. Briefly. In the editorial department. Of course, I've seen him since. Parties and that. Lunch sometimes. I liked him—a lot. I think everybody liked him. He was that kind of man." That's another thing about talking to policemen—they make you prattle on like an idiot.

"Yesterday, how did he seem to you?"

"Perfectly normal, I thought. He did complain a bit about his financial problems, but that's par for the course. You can't run a good publishing house in Canada without having finan-cial problems. He seemed very healthy."

"Did you think he was at all depressed?"

"Depressed? No. Why?... You're not suggesting he committed suicide...?"

"I'm afraid it's possible he may have," Parr said gravely.

"I don't believe it!" Judith gasped. "He just wouldn't have." She stood up and turned her back to the policeman, swallowed hard, smoothed over her face and her voice. "Would you like a cup of coffee? The kettle just boiled."

"Please. If it's not too much trouble." He was grateful she had gone into the kitchen. There had been more than enough tears already. The wife had had a hysterical screaming fit, then fainted. That was while he was standing at the door. The son was there, visiting, a fortunate coincidence that saved Parr from having to lug the unconscious Mrs. Harris into her house. Besides, he could not have left Mrs. Harris on her own. Harris Jr. had accompanied him to the hospital to identify the body.

Judith came back with a tray.

"How did it happen?" she asked.

"He fell or jumped in front of a subway train at Rosedale. We don't know for sure which."

Judith sighed and took a long sip of hot coffee. He wouldn't have jumped—not George. He was such a fastidious man. Even if he had intended to kill himself, he would have chosen a much more genteel way. Pills, for example.

"And you're sure he didn't seem at all unusual yesterday? What did he talk about?"

"Himself, mostly. And books. He had great hopes that he could pull Fitzgibbon & Harris out of debt by the end of the year. He had a very good list coming up this Fall. He knew he had a big winner. There had been some lean years, but he thought they were now behind him. Of course he knew the company would never get rich, but being out of debt would have meant a lot to him."

"Would mean a lot to anybody," Parr said, mostly to himself. "Harris Jr. gave me the impression that the lean years were very lean indeed. Wasn't he into the bank for a couple of million or more?"

"About two. But George was hanging in. And, as I said, he was optimistic. He seemed sure of himself."

"Would it have been realistic for him to think that one good list—how many books is that?"

"I don't know. Maybe thirty-five…"

"Well, could those books alone have got him out of debt?"

"Point is *he* believed it. While he believed it, he had something to fight for, and while he had something to fight for, he would not have given up. Not George."

Parr didn't mind her getting angry. As long as she didn't cry. He sipped his coffee and nodded reassuringly.

"What time did you leave his office?"

"Around 9:30. We were going to continue the interview next week. I was to call him today and set up a time. He thought he would have a drink with Marsha Hillier and me this afternoon."

"Who?"

"Marsha Hillier—a publisher in New York. She's coming because it's my birthday." That's the second time she had brought up the birthday in less than half an hour. Last night she hadn't told her friends, now she insisted on telling the policeman. Perhaps early senility?

"I'm sorry."

Why was *he* sorry? It wasn't his birthday.

"Did you and Harris leave his office together?"

"No. He said he had some work to finish and phone calls to make. He had a lot to do still. He couldn't have been planning to kill himself."

Once Parr had collected his raincoat and she was alone, Judith lit her first cigarette of the day and poured herself a generous Bloody Mary.

"That's for you, George," she said as she took a sip. "You never liked long faces or dreary people and you were a firm believer in Bloody Marys before noon."

She tidied up the kitchen and the living room, then took out the two frozen Quiches Lorraine she had been saving for a special occasion. They would defrost slightly by late afternoon.

It might be wise to invest in a dishwasher, she thought. Kids didn't like washing dishes any more than she did. If only she could get a big enough assignment, she might even prevail on the plumber to come and they'd have two working toilets again. You couldn't revel in such luxuries on $1,500 a month— when the going was good—and two growing kids. That's another thing: at fourteen and sixteen, respectively, shouldn't they stop growing soon? It would make a hell of a difference to the clothes budget. Even if Jimmy enjoyed having his jeans in tatters, he did like them to reach his ankles.

Hard as she tried to fill it with trivia, her mind kept returning to George Harris. What in heaven's name would he have been doing on the subway late at night? What, now that she thought of it, would he be doing on the subway at any time? George drove a car. His office was nowhere near the subway line. He never traveled by subway. Not even in dire straits. Hell, when the company was almost bankrupt, he still took first-class air tickets. Always a man with a sense of style. If he couldn't drive, he'd get a cab. He'd walk, for chrissakes! Worst came to the worst, he'd stay where he was. Let them come to him. Strange how the failure of his business to make money had affected George. The poorer the firm became, the more style he got.

She took out her interview notes which, as usual, were copious. Out of two hours with George Harris, she had recorded over thirty pages of tightly packed shorthand.

She had read through the first twenty when the managing editor of *Saturday Night* called. Had she heard the news, and could she get the story in by the end of the week? Now that George had died, there would be a number of stories. Hers was farthest ahead and they wanted it for the next issue. She said she would try, though she didn't think she could pull it together so quickly, at least not while there was any question of suicide.

The managing editor was quite convinced that they shouldn't probe into the suicide theory. The family wouldn't want that to be a topic of public discussion. They were entitled to *some* privacy.

After she had hung up, Judith finished reading her notes. Just as she remembered, George had been positively ebullient, really enthusiastic about the future. A few years ago he had had to restrain the publishing list, but those had been hard times in all spheres of business. Now he felt his debts were manageable. He anticipated that the whole industry would benefit from the federal government's new policy paper, and his firm, strong in its history of support for Canadian talent, would undoubtedly benefit the most. He planned to go to the American Booksellers' Association convention this year, for the first time in seven, because he had some important properties to discuss with American publishers. And he had just accepted an invitation to be the luncheon speaker at the annual meeting of the Canadian Authors' Association in Vancouver. He was going to talk about the importance of publicity for the success of a book and had a number of jokes and personal anecdotes already sketched out.

Would a man who was about to kill himself be inventing jokes?

Chapter Three

Now that she saw how miserable Judith looked, Marsha wished she'd been able to come last night, but Jelinek had staged an auction for Reginald Montgomery's new multi-generational saga, and Marsha had to be in on the bidding. It had opened at 4:00 p.m. with a floor price of $50,000, not an unhealthy start by Morrow (she guessed it was Morrow; the agent would sooner have sat on a hot griddle than reveal any names) and risen to $88,000 by 5:30. At 6:00 Jelinek had suggested she stop screwing around, which was his way of saying that the bidding was not going as high as he had in mind, but he noted her offer of $5,000 up anyway. The second round took over an hour. Marsha was ready with $100,000 when Jelinek called again, but they were at $120,000 already.

She had been obliged to call in Marketing for help. That meant giving young Markham a chance to parade his opinions while she forced herself to listen. She knew he had been waiting to be consulted because he had two sheets of statistics clutched to his chest, including sales figures for books she had never encountered. It was 6:30 and he had been waiting in his office for the phone to ring. Ambition without talent is a terrible thing, Marsha thought, but Larry Shapiro had insisted she call Markham if the price went over $100,000, and she had so much wanted to land Montgomery.

It wasn't over until 9:00. She'd lost the bidding and her temper at $150,000, Markham was still talking strategy, and it was too late to catch the last flight to Toronto.

She picked up the flowers on the way to La Guardia this morning, having guessed Judith would deny it was her birthday, so that there wouldn't have been any flowers yesterday. They were only daffodils, a perky glowing yellow, but they would brighten Judith's living room gloom. Marsha could never understand why Judith had stayed in this house after her divorce. Surely, she could have found something less dreary, even if she believed remaining in the neighborhood was essential for the kids. Too many changes would unsettle their delicate minds, Judith's mother had insisted. Marsha knew what the little lady really wanted was a restoration of the marriage. Even though it was James who had walked out, Mrs. DeLisle concluded Judith had been at fault. That was mostly what she decided about everything.

Marsha held Judith at arm's length, grinning, the daffodils between them. "How is the big girl today? Don't look a day over thirty, if you ask me. Not that it matters. Older is better. It's gentler, they say, more understanding. You'll love it."

"I hate it," Judith mumbled into Marsha's shoulder as they hugged each other.

"Did you ever think we'd make forty?" Marsha laughed. "Did you? No? That means you're doing better than you thought. Not even halfway through if you discount the years you're trying to forget…"

"I'm trying to forget last night and this morning."

"Too much celebration?"

"Too many martinis…"

"You're entitled."

"… and then George Harris died." Now Judith was crying into Marsha's shoulder.

"George Harris died?"

"Last night. Jeez, I'm getting your blouse wet. Come on in. I'm afraid I won't be much fun today..." She wiped her eyes on the back of her hand, exactly as she had used to when they were growing up together at Bishop Strachan School for girls, and told Marsha about her interview with Harris and about the policeman.

Marsha had known George for years, not closely. She had admired his enthusiasm, his willingness to take chances, and to push his authors with the Americans, who remained breezily unreceptive. She had made time for him when he came to New York and called on him when she was in Toronto. She had even allowed herself to be talked into publishing some of his authors, not because she always agreed with his assessment of their unsurpassed talents but because she had decided to back his judgment. He had often been right.

"Shit. He could have chosen a better time to do it." Marsha tried to snap Judith out of her gloom. "But I'm not going to let him ruin the whole day. Let's go to that ritzy restaurant you promised me, I want to treat you to something sumptuous—like carpaccio and zabaglione, and linguini with cream. You said it was Italian, didn't you?"

Marsha selected the dress and the shoes. She brushed Judith's hair and distracted her with David Markham and the auction.

"He actually believes in five-year strategic planning and comparative financial analysis, he refers to books as units and authors as elements, and he only laughs when he doesn't mean to. He whinnies if you ask him a question he hasn't anticipated."

"Why do you put up with him?"

"Larry hired him. He thinks we need some fresh thinking about marketing. He's fresh all right, wet-behind-the-ears fresh... I think he's angling for VP by next year."

In the event they had linguini with red wine and radicchio salad, and Judith told Marsha it wasn't going to work out with Allan Goodman, after all. OK for occasional companionship, but no point fooling herself there was any magic.

"Magic is fine for a month, kid, but it has no staying power. It's whether you can joke about making love when you wake up in the morning, and both laugh. *That's* the real magic."

"Allan is scientific about making love, and he doesn't think that's funny."

"I don't think my mother and father ever laughed together. About anything. He probably wore his vest to bed to make damned sure she wasn't going to touch him. I don't know how they managed to produce me; in those days there was no artificial insemination. I can't imagine them in bed together."

"You never could," Judith said. "Some thoughts we are never old enough for."

"Like what?"

"Understanding our parents."

They both had zabaglione, and Marsha gave Judith her birthday present: a round-trip ticket to New York for the coming weekend.

"It's what you wanted. We'll go to the theater. Have brunch at the Sherry-Netherland. We'll go back to the Frick."

"I have to finish my George Harris story. Now he's dead they want it in a week. You know, Marsha, he *couldn't* have planned to kill himself."

"Then get an extension and find out why he changed his mind. It'll make for a better story. But give it a rest for the weekend. You write better after a rest. Remember your group therapy story? It was fabulous."

"Yeah. I got sued."

"Nobody sues over boring stories."

"I don't know. It's hard to get away—with the kids…"

"Come on, they'd be glad to be alone for the weekend and you know it. Let your mother loose on them for mealtimes. They'll forgive you by the time they're thirty-eight."

"I still have the Nuclear Madness story to finish…"

"The one about closing the plant in Pickering?"

"And Whitby. It's $1,500. For the *Globe Magazine*."

"Not enough. Besides, it'll wait, and I can't. I'm in London the weekend after."

In the afternoon Marsha was going to visit M & A's Canadian subsidiary in Don Mills. She had to review the upcoming summer promotions and be back in New York in the evening. There was a reception for a British expert on contemporary papal diplomacy and its role in maintaining world peace. The event promised to be dreary but she had given Peter Burnett her word that she would attend. The expert was one of Peter's touring authors.

Judith was glad she hadn't asked Marsha about Jerry. Why spoil a perfectly pleasant lunch?